Gallery Books
Editor: Peter Fallon
TALES FROM THE POORHOUSE

Eugene McCabe

TALES
FROM THE
POORHOUSE

Gallery Books

Tales from the Poorhouse
is first published
simultaneously in paperback
and in a clothbound edition
on 22 April 1999.

The Gallery Press
Loughcrew
Oldcastle
County Meath
Ireland

*All rights reserved. For permission
to reprint these stories
write to The Gallery Press.*

© Eugene McCabe 1999.

The moral right of the author
has been asserted.

ISBN 1 85235 248 5 (*paperback*)
     1 85235 249 3 (*clothbound*)

The Gallery Press acknowledges the financial assistance
of An Chomhairle Ealaíon / The Arts Council, Ireland,
and the Arts Council of Northern Ireland.

Contents

The Orphan *page* 11
The Master 35
The Landlord 71
The Mother 106

I was revising an old play when Louis Lentin 'phoned: 'How about a quartet or sextet of individual stories set in a Famine poorhouse?'

I said, 'Yes, I'd like to try,' and thereby hang these tales.

E McC

*for Ruth
with love
and gratitude*

The Orphan

When the hard hunger reached us the Mother went half cracked blamin' Dada for near everythin', the landlord, the agent, the pig dyin', the leaky thatch, even the blight itself. Once when the run-off from the dungheap overflowed to the well she accused it made our Micilín sick. The truth is far different I'd say. It was her cuffin' and scoldin', then smotherin' the wee cratur with kisses, did some of the harm. Sadder again, Dada stood by. The man was too weakly to face up to her and then he couldn't look at us hungry, and the worse things got the worse she got, tongued and tongued and tongued. Betimes there were screechin' matches so awful me and Grace my twin sister put our two fingers in our two ears and ran away from the house and hid down in the sheugh that divides our ten acres from Noel Callaghan's land.

The Mother was all outshow and pride. What would the priest and the neighbours think of her two daughters were near hoors out dancin' and gallivantin' like mad heifers in heat and half the parish half dead from hunger? It was nothin' to her we were young and wanted our bit of life away from misery. She cared mostly for Micilín, God help him. He was forever coughin'. She kept him in a bag skirt to fool the fairies, but sure the fairies could see him at the back door holdin' his wee man to make his pee. Every bit of love and special care in our house went into that sick boy. She slept with him above in the cockloft over the byre.

One night when we came in late Dada was sittin' alone on the settle bed in the kitchen sayin' the same thing over and over. He was fair drunk I suppose. He said there was no way we'd get through the winter alive without a spud kind and every bird and beast about the place long gone. We'd be better off without him. There would be that much more to eat for the rest of us. Grace cried and begged him not to leave. I was upset too, but mostly stayed quiet.

He kept shakin' his head. He was a countryman's tailor but people had long since quit liftin' the latch. Like every other trade there was no money, only the promise of money. At fairs and gatherin's he was often, he said, at a loss. Men would order a swallow-tailed coat maybe, or britches, or a workin' waistcoat, and never come back to the lodgin's he worked out of. Then the Mother would say,

—That's your story, Tom Brady!

Then she'd tackle in to say he drank the money.

—What customer'd pay for clothes so illmade a monkey wouldn't wear them for fear of bein' laughed at!

Or she'd shout at him other times,

—You'll not shame me before the whole country!

No matter what any of us done we were shamin' her before the whole country! No one ever told her 'the whole country' doesn't know or care if you're alive or dead; no one in the country gives an ass's fart for anyone only themselves, and any halfwit could tell you that, and the same halfwit could tell you there's not a family in all Ireland hasn't some shame to hang its head about.

God knows me and Grace didn't want to think it but Dada was a poor enough tailor. When he come to this townland of Drumlanna twenty years back the Mother was long past thirty.

The Orphan

By all accounts they were happy enough in the early years with a bit of land and the tailorin'. It was she calved and milked the cow, cut and footed the turf, put in and dug out the spuds, but when the blight came and rotted them in the ground the cow had to be sold. Then the fowl were eaten and when the hard hunger came she'd scream at him,

—You have a wife and three childer to feed now, Tom Brady. Have you no shame to be gulpin' and pissin' the most of it in a ditch! It's horsewhipped you should be, you and drunkards like you!

Then he'd leave the house for days. When he'd come back we could tell he was drinkin' from his dead eyes and senseless talk. Thing is, he could measure, cut and sew, but he was careless or maybe the drink would put a tremble in his fingers and that made a *prácás* of the work he was at. When a customer was tryin' on we could see it was wrong and if that happened he'd give the garment a tug or twist and say there was poor give in the cloth.

—It'll warm into your body, he'd say.

What put the Mother astray in the head was the way he mostly wouldn't talk back. When she tongued he just stood there and looked at the floor.

Not long before he left us for good Lord Clonroy sent for him. The Viceroy Lord Clarendon had arrived at Eden Hall with a bolt of Donegal tweed under his arm. He wanted a pair of shootin' britches made. Dada brought the cloth home and worked all day and all night and terrible nervous he was because the great man was left-handed and left-handed men are hung opposite to right-handed men so everythin' had to be made the other way about.

When he brought the britches to Eden Hall they were all at dinner, full of wine and good humour. The Viceroy went into another room and came back in wearin' the britches.

No one said a thing at first. Then Lord Clonroy said,
—I'll tell you what you've done, Brady. You've made a bags of the Viceroy's britches!

They all thought that was so funny they near laughed themselves sick except the Viceroy. This is where me and Grace differ. She had tears in her eyes on account of the way Dada was shamed, took his hand, kissed it and said,
—That was terrible for you, Dada.

I was filled with so much anger I wanted to hit him and walk out of the house. That kind of self sorry whinge makes me sick to my stomach. Small wonder he loved Grace more than he loved me and maybe that made me jealous a track, but not all that much. The truth is I loved her too much to be mad jealous.

Anyway he went on with his story. In the middle of all the laughin' the Viceroy crossed the room, took Dada's arm and went out to the great hall. He asked him how many childer he had, were there grandparents in the house? Had we any spuds at all, and what other food was there in the house or garden? And how was it with our neighbours? Dada told him the hard hunger was on us, that all our neighbours were the same as us.
—The people, your honour, are starvin', and that's the truth.

The Viceroy repeated that in Irish, put his hand up to his mouth and made a wee hummin' noise. Then he took a golden guinea out of his purse and pressed it on Dada.
—No, no, your Lordship, Dada said, that's a ransom for bad made britches.
—The britches, the Viceroy said, are grand.
—The man's a born gentleman, Dada said, every inch of him. I'd follow him to hell if he gave me the nod.

The Mother we all thought deep asleep above in the cockloft with Micilín. She must have heard 'cause all of a sudden she spoke,

The Orphan

—It's the like of that fine born gentleman has made a hell out of this whole island.

We stared up at her. You could see Dada didn't understand till she said,

—And it's the like of you, Tom Brady, has made a hell out of this house with your booze and your blether. Let you show your dotin' daughters now what's left of the great lord's hansel.

The Mother's temper is worse than any storm. He had no choice. He had sixteen shillings and a few pence left, enough to feed us all for a month. He had drunk near a week's food and though we loved him we all felt angry and ashamed about this. The Mother had come down from the cockloft. We watched her countin' the money. She went over then to where Dada was sittin' on the settle bed, put her head down sideways and shouted into his face five or six times,

—Fool, fool, fool, fool, fool, fool!

Each time it was like she'd slapped him with her open hand across the face and then she was half-gulpin', half-chokin' as she cried out,

—We'll all starve to death here, Tom Brady, because I married a fool.

That was the night he left and never come back, no message, nothin'. And when I think now of the differ between that man, our father, and that woman, our mother, I have to say Grace was more like him. She couldn't stand up for herself. She was soft. She'd cry over a sick kitten or a dead chicken or a silly story. I was well able to cry myself but I'd near die before I'd let anyone see me. But I pray God I won't end up like the Mother. I heard Dada mutter once,

—It's not hunger'll kill that woman, it's pride!

No matter how hungry we were she'd always have bought soap in the house or if there was no money she'd make it herself.

—Water costs nothin', she'd say, and by God you girls'll keep your bodies clean and your souls pure as long as you're in my care.

She smelled of carbolic herself and made sure we did too. It was out to the turfshed every mornin', summer and winter, with the tin jug and basin, teeth first with soot, then strip down while she watched to make sure we'd wash neck, ears, back passage and up between our legs, and there was stuff in that soap went up into you like a bee sting. Then dry yourself with a hessian bag and, the only good thing, it gave us chance to see what the other looked like because no one could tell us apart. What I saw, Grace saw. Eyes and hair black as sloes above a heron's neck, shapely legs goin' up to her lovepurse and the rise of her bottom, and a heather dye you'd swear round her brown nipples, and all her skin as white as her teeth.

—Why does she put us through that washin' 'torture'? Grace asked once.

—Because we smell young and natural, I said. She hates that. Snig off our rosebuds if she had her way and tell us the Devil put them in there to make us sin.

When I'd say the like she'd laugh, bite her lip and say,

—God forgive you, Rosh.

I was the first born and had a hard time comin' into the world or so I was often told. Maybe that's what made me harder than Grace in my head and heart or so I imagine but none of that matters anymore. Dada left that night after she shouted fool at him so wicked vicious, and hardly a day passes or a night but I think of him. How or where did he die? Who buried him? Where? Ditch, bog or mountain place? Did he throw himself in a deep river or the sea like so many? If that's what fell out I'll have to think of him as gone to God's light or the Devil's dark

The Orphan

or is he maybe alive somewhere up about Dundalk or Dublin? They say the hunger's as bad in the towns as the country and anyway who'd employ a poor tailor only the poor and the poor have nothin'. He's dead I think with a million others.

When the Mother found him gone the next day it wasn't tears came out of her two eyes but bad temper out of her mouth.

—A rotten match my own father made for me with Tom Brady. What good's my stone thatched cabin and ten acres with a poor breed of man drunk in the chimbley corner, a class of coward runs out on his whole family when trouble comes.

Then because she had no man to cut with her tongue she grigged us about every other thing we did or said. So we kept away from the house every chance we got. And why not! Weren't we young girls out for a bit of life and who could blame us with death every other day in every other townland? At night we'd lie close and talk and giggle about the boys and the kind of them, who was good for a coort, and who was shy, and who we'd let and how far we'd let them. Then one night Grace asked me,

—Did ever you let a fella proper?
—Close enough, I said.
—I let Jimmy Ned O'Hara.
—You did not, Grace!
—God help I did.
—You're mad in the head.
—I know.
—Why?
—He cried, Rosh.
—What!
—Cried, wept and gulped like a babby.
—For why?
—For me to let him in. Said he'd die if I said no.

—Well isn't Jimmy Ned the quare cute one! I'd say you're not the first lassie he's cried for!
—I know.
Then she started in to cry to herself, so I put my two arms around her and kissed away her fright. Then I lay awake long after she'd gone to sleep. I couldn't take in what she'd told me about herself and Jimmy Ned. She was ahead of me in the biggest thing happens to a girl. She was a woman now even if the way it happened was silly enough. I couldn't take it in rightly. I looked and looked at her face asleep. Not the smallest change, but it was a woman's face I was lookin' at and I thought I can't be such a nice creature to have jealous thoughts about the person I love most in the world and who loves me even more than she loves herself. From the time we were wee things I could see nothin' in that face but admiration. She was fierce proud of me. I'd hear her boastin' about me to others, how I could run and jump and wrestle and best any boy my own size.

It never seemed to come into her head that me bein' better at everythin' cast her into a kind of shade. She loved bein' my sister and I had to admit to myself she had more nature, more heart, more kindness and goodness, more gentleness and warmth than me, and then I became so upset thinkin' about how much better she was than me at everythin' that mattered that I began to be sorry for myself. She woke up, put her two arms around me and said,

—Roisin, Roisin, don't you be sorry for me, I'll be alright, I'll be alright.

I couldn't tell her it wasn't for her I was cryin' but for myself, and that made me all the more miserable.

As luck would have it she was far from alright. Life began to waken in her belly from the crybaby boy, and one mornin' after the stirabout, when she left in a hurry

The Orphan

to get sick, didn't the Mother see her and know right off. Then there was a screechin' match to end all screechin' matches. She took Grace up to the cockloft by the ear, put a cow's chain round her neck and closed it tight with a blacksmith's pincers. Then she nailed the end of the chain to the roofbeam with nails as big as the ones they used on Christ and kept her up there with a bowl and a bucket. We were too young and too frightened to know what to do. With Dada long gone, no money, nothin' in the house but ten days of stirabout, nothin' in our fields but cabbage stumps and nothin' but a cock's step between us and the poorhouse I began to wonder what I could do to get money in my fist to feed us all.

Lord Clonroy had a twenty-acre turnip field over the estate wall that marched Drumlanna, our wee garden of a farm. The turnips were long since dug by squads of men to feed sheep and bullocks. Twice the Mother let me out to cross the wall and glean at night. Each time I came back with a bag of crow-pecked, half-frosted roots. The Mother fried them with a little pig fat. They were so delicious they made our heads light. Each time in the black dark I could hear the German wolfdogs over a mile away up at the big house. They were kept in a special yard alongside the prize cattle and sheep penned in every night for fear the gangs of Ribbonmen would slash their tendons. The third time out I got braver. There was a moon and I went a long way from the estate wall out into the middle of the field. I was hokin' and gatherin' rightly when I heard first the chains and then the growlin' of wolfdogs. They must have smelled me and for a few seconds of terror my heart stopped entirely. I could hear a henchman shoutin',

—Gwon, gwon, gettim, boy, gettim!

I knew that Wishy Mulligan's throat was ripped out by those dogs. Then I was runnin' as I'd never run in my life and was over that wall a brave few minutes before the dogs came howlin' up to where I'd crossed. The fright was bad but the loss of the turnips was worse. The Mother had to hear all and said she'd have near died of shame if one of her daughters was caught clawin' like a starved rat in the dark of an empty landlord's turnip field.

Not long after this, Mervyn Johnston, the warden of the ten townlands, came to visit us, a Protestant gentleman with over a hundred acres. He spoke Irish like us and most people said he was kindly and helpful, but for the Mother the word Protestant meant he had cloven feet and horns.

—You can't see them but they're there.

So when he said he thought he could place one of us in the scullery of the big house, if that would be any help, the Mother said,

—You can send your own daughter for a scullion, Mr Johnston, you'll not get mine.

And even with that said to his face he answered quiet,

—If you change your mind, Mam, just let me know.

Not get mine! Hers to give! Body and soul! Does the mad, proud woman of Drumlanna own her two daughters and her sick son?

—Oh, she didn't mean it that way, Grace said.

—How then so did she mean it? What does that chain round your neck mean?

And of course she had no answer to that. From the time we were small I could always talk her into a knot she couldn't unknot except with a protest.

—God you're a fright, Roisin.

—And I'll stay one if it keeps us alive, I said.

It was the night I had to race from the turnip field that I lay awake thinkin' how from the age of twelve I could run faster than any other girl or boy I knew, but what good was runnin' to get bread? Then it came to me that

The Orphan

gentry will pay money to see boxin' matches, and wager money on hounds, cocks and coursin' hares, and at the field day sports Lord Clonroy would give prize money for runnin' and jumpin' but that was only one day in the year when you could show your paces. It was that spake, 'Show your paces', that gave me a mad idea. At horse fairs the seller always had to show the paces of the horse he was sellin', and watchin' this I used to think, I could run as fast as that horse, faster, and then I thought how every other day there were grand visitors to Eden Hall would have fat purses of money. I could run alongside the carriage no matter how fast it went. They'd see me and think, 'She'll tire, she can't go on'. Then after half a mile they'd have to look at me and if they had any breedin' they'd throw me out a coin or maybe somethin' from a hamper or maybe a rug I could pawn. But if I got nothin' I'd lost nothin' and I hadn't begged. So I watched my chance, climbed the wall a good bit down from the gate-keeper's lodge where Ivan Dowler lived. As luck would have it, I saw a carriage a long way off. That gave me time to get down and run to a bend of the avenue where I stood behind one of the great lime trees that marched on either side all the way up to the big house.

When the carriage came level I began to run ahead of the horses. The coachman Clancy let a roar at me to get to hell out of the way. I obeyed him, moved to the side, and let the coach draw alongside. He roared again,

—Get off the earth!

I paid no heed knowing well that whoever was inside the coach must see me now and wonder what I was at, a girl of seventeen runnin' as easy as a runnin' dog. I was careful not to turn my head and look into the carriage but I heard a young man's voice say,

—Faster, Clancy.

I still didn't look but I increased my pace to keep up

with the slow gallop of the horses knowin' I could go ahead of them if I wanted. Then I heard three more words from the same voice,
—The whip, Clancy.
—To her or the horses, Master?
—The horses, man, the horses!

I was sorry then for the way the knotted thongs cut the poor creatures. I could see foam at their mouths and smell the sweet smell of horse sweat. I was still runnin' easy enough, and plenty left.

The big house was still over half a mile away. At a downhill stretch the carriage drew level. From the corner of my eye I could see three young men and two young ladies inside. I knew one of the young men was Mathew, Lord Clonroy's only son. He leaned out the window and made a gesture with his hand which meant, 'Go away'. I paid no heed, then heard him shout above the clatter of wheels and hooves,
—You'll burst your lungs, girl, go home!

At that very moment I felt blood on my thighs and knew what had happened. Then something caught my foot. I fell down on my face. I knew they had all seen me fall but if they did they saw me get up as quick. I was still level but now my nose was bloody. I was half glad of that because maybe they'd only see that and not the other. Inside in myself I felt I was like a childeen who'd fallen and can't get breath because the hurt is so painful. I was tempted to stop but I must have that pride my mother has.

I'll keep runnin', I thought, till someone throws out somethin'. Just when it was hardest with the big house and the lake in view I heard a coin sing on the stone of the avenue. Then another. Then another. Then another. Then another. Five sixpences. Enough to buy two weeks' India meal. I stopped. The carriage drew away. My

The Orphan

hands, in truth my whole body, were tremblin'. There was a taste of blood and sweat in my mouth. I went straight off the avenue into a copse of oak trees and sat on the ground. I realised then I could hardly breathe.

When it got easier I was cryin'. I cried a brave bit while I wiped my nose and thighs with moss and tried to think why I was whingein' like a two-year-old. Hadn't I two full shillin's and sixpence in the linin' of my shift? Maybe it was the relief of knowin' we could hold off from the poorhouse a while longer and I hadn't held out my hand to whine like a beggar. I'd run proud with my head up, but I'd fallen. Dear Jesus, I'd fallen on my mouth and nose and maybe it was that fall and the knowledge of what was happenin' below under the eyes of high bred young men and women. Through my patched rags they must have seen the bareness of poverty. Was that what caused them to drop out the biteens of silver?

I burned with shame thinkin' of this. Would I, could I, do the same again if I had to, two weeks from now? I was thinkin' these thoughts when I saw Ivan Dowler, the gatelodge keeper, the worst breed of henchman, come into the oak copse carryin' his whitethorn stick. He had frog eyes and the low hung lip of a bully.

Did someone tell him how I'd raced the carriage and braved Clancy's whip? I'm not sure what come over me, maybe hundreds of years of bein' wronged, but somewhere from my lungs I screamed at him so loud it near frightened me as much as him. Then I let another and another till the screamin' became more like the howlin' of a trapped creature through clenched teeth. I could see that he had stopped and could hear him growl,

—Quit, quit that. Quit!

Then of a sudden I was gone.

How long I was lyin' there I've no notion. I know only I was chilled through and through when I woke and so stiff I could scarce move. Did that landlord's brute come up and stare, then walk away and leave me there like a creel of rubbish? As I sat up I heard a foxbitch give her wee sharp bark and I thought if she can feed and rear her litter with all the world agin' her, why can't I take care for my mad, proud mother, my pregnant sister and my sick brother? I can.

The first stars were about the sky when I got home and the Mother waitin' for me like black thunder till I took the five sixpences from the hem of my shift. She looked into the cup of my hand and her face was two faces, one lit up because we'd eat, the other with a twist on her mouth which said,

—You begged, daughter?
—I ran.
—You what!
—I ran.
—Liar!
—I ran against Lord Clonroy's carriage. I never spoke, I never looked, I ran and they dropped out silver.

She seemed too stunned to understand and muttered,
—That's beggary.

She was so desperate she asked no more, snatched the silver and went to Dermody's for meal and fat. I went up to Grace in the cockloft. She had the white face of a half-starved girl with a child growin' in her belly. We were all like ghosts but she was by far the poorest and whitest of ghosts. I put my two arms around her and every bit of me loved every bit of her and I kept sayin' how I loved her and how she'd be alright and how her babby would be alright and maybe someway I'd get the money and we'd have a new life in America. All the roads of Ireland, I said, were full of the poor of Ireland walkin' to the ports. In America there would be no Kings or Queens, no agents or landlords, no bailiffs or house tumblers.

The Orphan

We'd be welcomed by our own people into a new world. There would be food and clothes, singin' and dancin', proper work and proper wages in a country where we'd be all free at last.

I knew in my heart of hearts that none of this was true, not lies, but not true. Even so, I kept sayin' it again and again and again. Then she had to know how I got the money and when I told her my story I could see her eyes gettin' bigger and bigger and her mouth openin' in wonder.

—Gawdy! If I fell down that way I'd stay down.

She was speakin' the truth about herself, but sittin' on that bag of rushes with that chain around her neck I knew the round of her belly was a chain could never be loosened except by death, and again I began to badmouth the Mother even though that always upset her.

—She loves us, Roisin.

I pointed at the chain and asked,

—Is that love?

—She's sick with worry over the head of everythin'.

—She's mad with pride, or just plain mad.

Again Grace looked away for a while and then said,

—It was me that sinned, Rosh. Me, not her.

I made no answer to that silliness. The Mother was either mouthin' prayers or usin' a tongue would cut you in two. I knew Rosh half believed what she preached, that Holy God had sent down the blight and the hard hunger to punish us for all our sins of impurity.

—Three Hail Marys, she'd say, for this, that and the other, every other half hour of the night or day and we'd have to answer,

—Holy Mary, Mother of God, pray for us sinners now and at the hour of our death.

Night and day it's sinners and death. Death the last word in that prayer. Every time death, death, death, death, death, death, death, death, death, death. Ten deaths with every decade. Thousands everywhere now, in every townland of every barony of every province, sick from sin, Godstruck unto death. And thousands of poor halfwits and unlucky girls like Rosh locked up, tied or chained in lofts, sheds or sties, hidin' their shame from God and the neighbours. Jesus, God, are You as cruel as that? Are You?

—Holy, holy, holy, Lord God of hosts, heaven and earth are full of Thy glory.

When the time come for the babby to be born the Mother gagged Grace for fear she'd cry out with the pains and the neighbours would hear. I was kept out. I stood in the dark listenin' and cryin'.

No midwife. The babby was a day and a night comin' into the world and when I heard its wee cry I couldn't think how it would be suckled in a house with a grandmother hated it, so I did a mad thing, God help me. I ran away from our house to John Joseph Duffy. I crossed four townlands in the dark till I reached the lock-keeper's cottage. I tapped on his window and told him the way things were above in Drumlanna and that I wanted us to be man and woman that night. And we were, in the cabin of a barge called 'The Rose of Mooncoyne'. Three times that night we cried out together and I don't know to this day why it had to be that night and that way, and I don't know now if he's alive or dead or taken up with another or sendin' the passage money he promised in a letter he sent on his way to America.

It was near daylight when I got back to Drumlanna to hear a terrible story. God help me, I can't hardly let into my head what dark things were done after I left. It's all between God and my poor mother in the idiot ward of the poorhouse.

Grace was stretched dead as any dead thing you'd see in a ditch or a bog. It was a great flood of bleeding did it.

The Orphan

I saw after where the blood dripped down through the cockloft to the group of the byre below.

—The babby, she said, was dead born. It made no shape to breathe at all, only a wee gurgle.

—Was it a boy or a girl? I asked.

—What matters that to you? You weren't here wherever you were. It's dead. When I'm at myself you'll answer to me where you were till this hour.

—Where is the wee thing buried?

—It's with God.

And she went straight to Micilín in the settle bed where he was coughin' like a sick cat. When they were both asleep I went up and cried my eyes dry beside Grace. I thought of the way we'd walk together, my arm around her neck and her arm around my waist, and all the silly talk we made and all the laughin' and betimes the cryin', about everythin' and nothin', and I knew lookin' at her I'd never love any creature in the world the way I loved my sister.

When I was fit to cry no more I went out to look for where the *bábóg* was buried. I wasn't long in findin' it. I could see where she'd prised up a flagstone in the byre. I did the same and there was a Lisnaskea butter box and inside the box the babby with a terrible red ring on its neck from the rope its grandmother used to put it out of the world forever. A wee girl it was, and I can't tell you why that made it worse, but it did.

It was rage then I felt for this woman would sicken you with her moanin' and her prayers and her rosaries, her saints, pishogues and fairies. She had murdered her own flesh and blood and I was her daughter, the daughter of a murderer, and her so proud of her kin, the grand Daly blood she had in her veins compared to the poor, thin Brady blood in Dada's veins. It's true he got drunk betimes but if he did he told us funny stories, showed us card tricks, never hit or cuffed us the way she did, and never a bad word out of his mouth about anybody, not even the landlords.

—And sure maybe they have their own troubles, he'd say, and people would look at him as if he was mad.

Aloud in that byre I said,

—Dada, she's murdered your granddaughter. You're well out of it.

It was midday before the priest, Brendan Galligan, came on his horse with his top hat and his horsewhip. He said the settle bed should be sold to buy a cheap coffin. Then he said his few prayers and sprinkled holy water on Grace and the way that woman bleated after him, Father this, Father that, and Father the other, and the whole carry on of her, you'd swear Jesus Christ Himself was in the house and not one word about chains and cocklofts and buckets and chokin' a babby to death. Then he turned to me,

—A sad day this but it must be said, both you girls have disgraced our parish, one worse than the other. This death is a judgement of God on your mad capers.

—Oh God help us, said the Mother, but it's the truth you've spoken, Father.

I kept my mouth shut and he went on,

—The whole country knows about your dancin' and what you get up to in barns and ditches. You've put a lot of decent young men astray in the head and the whole country half starved. It's wicked beyond words. I'm certain sure it was the burden of shame drove your poor father out of his own house.

I stared down at my two bare feet and made not one word of an answer.

—Have you nothin' to say for yourself, girl?

Then I looked at his grand shiny boots, and the shine of good feedin' on his face and the proud stance of him,

The Orphan

and the belly on him like there were twins in it at least, and wondered the way any girl would was he all shrivelled up in there or hung like a stallion ass. Then I looked straight into his two eyes and I thought for a minute he'd hit me with his horsewhip, but he took a big breath and said,

—It's to God you'll have to answer, girl, God, not me.

He was hardly out the door when the Mother slapped me hard across the face and if she did I slapped her back so quick and sudden she fell back against the crook of the hearth and I said to her,

—True as God, woman, if you hit me again I'll kill you dead because it's dead you should be.

And I picked up the pincers she'd used to close the cow-chain on Grace's neck.

—God and His holy Mother, protect me, says she, what have I done to deserve this?

—What have you not done? You know well what you've done. You're the Devil's own now.

She knew I knew but not a word was said. When it came to the layin' out of Grace I was in such a fury of grief I wouldn't let her near. I sent for John Joseph. As he took her down the ladder from the cockloft with one arm her head was restin' on his shoulder the way I'd often seen her at a dance, that sudden lift and laugh as merry as a child's, and I could hardly see what I was at because it's myself I was layin' out and washin' for the last time and I remembered how elders often talked of the dead as bein' 'peaceful'.

—At peace, they'd say, at rest, happy now.

But Grace's face was a way I'd never seen it, her soft mouth a hard line across her clamped teeth. Rage? For youth and beauty cheated? For what? Pride.

It fair sickened me watchin' the Mother after the keenin' was over and the grave filled bendin' her head to

neighbours, all of them lettin' on to know nothin' and knowin' or guessin' everythin'.
—She's gone to Jesus.
—Cratur's with God's Mother now.
—She's an angel with angels.
And a dose of other holy sayin's put me mad angry or maybe it was the way the Mother muttered back,
—Aye, she's happy now in heaven surely.
I wanted to shout out like a whiplash through all the whisperin',
—She was chained to a roofbeam, she was terrified, and she died a cruel, bloody death, and that carbolic-smellin' woman with the pious face choked and buried her wee babby. She was in hell, my lovely, gentle sister, and is she now in heaven with Jesus? And if Jesus knew the carry on in our house why could He not shift Himself to help her? And for a bad minute I thought I'd shout out,
—It's a clip on the ear Jesus wants to waken Him up!
But I held my tongue, thank God.
The Mother was never in her right mind from that day out. If she heard the squeal of an owl or rabbit, the shriek of a swallow, or a hound howlin' at night, she'd think it was the babby she heard and start in to cry and wander the country prayin' and ravin' about two angels were lost and how she'd earn hell if they weren't found. It was the warden, Mervyn Johnston, found her naked in the bog of Scart, her whole body scrabbed by thorns and briars.
There's a shed here for mad women in the grounds of the poorhouse. That's where they put her. I saw her there just the once. I won't ever see her again. Leastways I don't want to. I thought I hated her but when I saw her in that ward I don't know what I felt. She was still clean, on clean straw, but surrounded by filth and smell, her

only company the gibberin' and laughin' of mad women night and day.

Her eyes were blank but her lips were movin'. Hail Mary, Holy Mary. Where did all those Hail Marys lead in the end but down the darkest road of all? Once for the smallest second I thought she twigged who I was but when I tried to look into her eyes she swivelled them off. I tried again. She did the same and then I saw the tell-tale tears and thought, she knows or half knows, remembers or half remembers, somethin' of that terrible night, and I knelt and took her hands and kissed them. Oh God, I kissed those hands and heard myself sayin',

—I can't forgive you, Mother, ever, you must know that.

She looked at me proper then for the first time, covered her face, no sound, but I could see her body shakin'. Some mad pauper woman started in to howl like a hound. Another joined her. That's how I left her in the hell she made for herself. That's when I saw her last and it's the last time I'll ever see her or less we meet in heaven, if God forgives her.

That left me and Micilín half alive and half dead in an empty house with hardly a crumb between the two of us.

A short time after this Mister Johnston came back to talk about the Mother and see how we were faring. He knew no neighbours could help out. We were all in the one boat and it goin' down.

When he saw Micilín out on the street in daylight I could tell from the way he blinked that things were bad. He sent for Doctor O'Grady who took me aside and said,

—The caudie has typhus, he's not long for this world.

I had to lean against the cabin wall when I heard this.

—You can't nurse him or go near him or you'll not be long after him.

Then he looked into the byre and showed me where Micilín was to lie on a bed of rushes near enough to where the *bábóg* was buried. I was to lock the door tight and seal it with blue clay and give him his stirabout and water on a shovel through the small windy, then close the windy tight and keep well away from infection.

—A dog would die of loneliness from the like of that, I said.

The only answer he made was to nod and say,

—When he dies it would be best to leave him in there and burn the byre.

I carried him out and laid him on rushes in the corner of the byre like I was told. He pleaded with me to get back into the cabin. I was sick with grief and pity but what could I do?

He never took a mouthful of stirabout or a porringer of water off the shovel, just sobbed, curled up, and stopped breathin'. Neighbours came then with sticks and creels of turf to make sure the byre was well burned. For three nights and three days it burned, and I wept bitter tears because all belongin' to me were now gone. I was an orphan like thousands and thousands the country over. Then Mister Johnston called again and out of his pocket he took a red book of tickets with numbers on them. He wrote my name on one and gave it to me.

—What's this for? I asked.

—The workhouse, Roisin, it's your only hope.

I looked at the red ticket in my hand with my name and number on it. At first I couldn't speak. When I was fit to I said,

—Hereabouts, Mister Johnston, people call this the death ticket. I'd rather die here where I was born.

He looked away for a while and then said,

—There's tumblin' talk.

—Is there?

The Orphan

—I heard them in the barracks, a squad from Mayo, and I've seen the list, Drumlanna's on it, next Thursday.

My heart and insides were suddenly tumblin' in terror. I'd seen the Callaghans, my cousins, evicted in the mouth of Christmas last year, five of them, the door smashed down, and what choice had they then but the workhouse or the killin' winter? They were carted off to the poorhouse, three of them now dead. I'd seen the tumblers at work, men from another county evicted themselves and now tumblin' out their own kin into cruel December. One jumps up and saws the roofbeam, the others throw up grapple hooks, and the roof is down in minutes. We saw the Constabulary sittin' on horseback watchin' with muskets and truncheons. Terror, fright and howlin' to break the hardest heart.

I looked again at the red ticket and he saw me lookin'.

—You've some kind of a chance in the workhouse, girl. Stay here and you've none.

I thanked him and said, no, I'd rather take to the fields and roads than go to the poorhouse.

—You're making a big mistake, he said.

He must have gone to Reggie Murphy, the workhouse master, who came out himself to persuade me. I'd never seen the man, but I'd heard tell a lot about him. With a name like that I was mad curious to know was he a Protestant or one of us. I found out soon enough. He'd no time for any class of religion. When he said a word or two in English it sounded the way the English talk but his Irish is without fault, a big easy man with a deep voice, well set up and for all the world like a bishop or gentry. He came on a horse but wore no hat. His clothes were the clothes of a fine gentleman. He's got bluey eyes like you'd see in a tinker's piebald, and the crinkly hair of a mountainy man.

They all say hereabouts he's a bad lad. If he takes a

notion of some girl or woman he'll buy her passage if she opens her legs for him. 'Tis said he ships paupers to America and the landlords pay him well for that and they say he has land leased from evicted paupers for next nothin' and fine bullocks fattenin' on it and a sty of pigs not far from the poorhouse. So! Hasn't every doctor, priest, merchant and auctioneer his own bit of land and sty of pigs? Sure what have the landlords behind their stone walls only a wee kingdom of birds and beasts, of fields and gardens? Isn't that how we all stay alive, the bit of land and the bit to eat?

When I told him my story a sort of mist came into his eyes and I thought to myself he can't be as bad as they all say. I'd prefer him a lot to the likes of Father Brendan Galligan with his bad temper and his threats of hell. He said he could find me fair to middlin' sleepin' quarters. I'd be off the stone floor. I'd be workin' in the kitchen. I'd bring his meals to his room. If I proved useful I might get some paid work. He then put his hands on my neck and felt my glands, made me open my mouth and looked down my throat. I felt like a filly at a horse fair. When he was at this I could see him lookin' down through my poor patched smock and I knew well what was in his head. A while back I'd have said, 'It's bad manners to stare at a girl like that' but I just said,

—I'll take the red ticket.

And that's what has me in this place. But I'll fight, I'll do anythin' to stay alive and, with luck, I'll get my hands on five golden guineas and get away to America, because no place in the world could be worse than this except hell itself, and no girl ever had to be shamed like me. But then look how fear of shame tumbled the Mother into hell, and anyway I knew well what to expect when I said,

—I'll take the red ticket.

The Master

How can I begin to explain what I scarcely understand myself? And how should I address you? My Dearest Anne Marie? That's too formal. My Dearest Sister? Not much better. Dear Annie? That's what I called you long ago in Calcutta where our father, Willie Murphy, was batman to General Lord Clonroy. We were the fourth generation of Murphys to be employed by that landed, Fermanagh family.

There were only the two of us: me (Lonan) and yourself. Father sometimes called you Mary Ann for a tease. Anne Marie, he said, was much too uppity for a batman's daughter and I have no idea what notion or fashion possessed them to brand me with Reginald as a second name.

I can still hear those bugles at dawn and the flapping of a flag the night I woke screaming about vultures in the quadrangle. Was that a forewarning? And always the smell of otherness from the surrounding streets. Do you remember the blind beggars, maimed children and mothers suckling infants at the barracks gates? Hungry looking and begging. Once, in the care of a servant on some errand, we saw a pack of dogs feasting on a bloated body thrown up by the river.

Is it not strange now with service bred in me how I can write that word 'servant' so easily? But then even batmen can hire house servants in India. She couldn't have been too responsible when she allowed us to stare like that at human degradation. And who would have thought such horror could ever visit this ancient island of ours so thronged with saints, so especially beloved of God Himself and His Blessèd Mother? Or so we've always been led to believe.

Small wonder we crept from our beds to Mother's bed for the comfort of whisperings in Irish in the cradle of her arms, the joy of her storytelling, and the way she'd laugh and kiss us turn about. She was love and protection we thought could never end. But it did, when an army doctor said quietly to Father,

—I'm afraid, Willie, it's more serious than sunstroke. Your poor wife has meningitis.

Then that night of vomiting, and she was gone. Sometimes I think of her across all that vastness of land and sea at the other end of the earth, lying in a military graveyard with no kin of her own to visit and talk kindly. Aboardship on the way back Father got so sick we weren't allowed to see him in sick bay and, when he died of dehydration, that knowledge was kept from you. They buried him at sea. That I did not witness but have dreamt of it a thousand times. Was it the grief of that double loss that's made me cold seeming to common compassion, indifferent almost to the dying I have to accommodate almost daily in this union of death?

I was eight at the time and too stricken to weep. You were three or four and kept asking,

—Lolo, when will we see Dada? When will Mama come back from heaven?

Finally I had to use that saddest of sad words,

—Never.

I can still see your eyes at Granard as Aunt Bridie carried you from coach to ass and cart without the smallest warning that we were to be parted. That transfer was so brutal seeming, so unexpected, that I've no memory of what our aunt looked like. All I remember is being alone and your calling out my pet name again and again.

—Lolo, Lolo, Lolo.

Afterwards I wept enough to do me a lifetime. That's thirty years ago now and during all that time I don't think I cried once till that black afternoon and the days following Lady's Day, the twenty-fifth of March. This memoir is intended to mark that date. It's an apology, Annie, part confession and part explanation for why I behaved as I did. A late and useless apology, but I'd like you to understand why I've become what I've become. In truth, I'm loath to recall and set down detail, but I'll try. Like all such accounts I may steer off truth by recalling everything but the one thing that overwhelmed me that afternoon and still does two weeks later.

After the wrench of Granard they brought me on here to Fermanagh where I was fostered out to people called Ferguson. Fostered or adopted? I'm not sure which, but there must be a difference. Sam and Hannah Ferguson of Derrylester. They had a valley farm in a sheltered townland under the Bragan mountains. It looked down on a twelve-acre lake. There was a crown of mature beech near the house and rows of tall hardwoods in the well-kept ditches. Decent, south-facing land it was, marched by a modest river, and a decent, childless Presbyterian couple they were. I was fond enough of them growing up though they never encouraged me to visit you on my way to or from school in Kilkenny. In truth I was neither dissuaded nor encouraged, but difficulties were implied. The coach would have to make a detour or I would have to overnight in Granard. A bit young for that on my own. Perhaps when I was older. From an early age you learn to read the hints and nods, the smiles and silences of what will, or will not, be approved.

And, although I thought of you from time to time, I still kept away long after I was free to travel. Would we recognise each other I wondered? What would we have in common? Blood, of course, but would you remember anything that far back? I knew I'd be welcomed as family, knew also that that can have drawbacks. Requests, I suspected, would follow: a pig, a cow, a dowry, something for someone's confirmation, fares to America, Australia. I'm as selfish as the next fellow, my life ahead. I knew indirectly that you were hired out in some midland town — Ferbane, Athlone, Mullingar — that you'd married, had a child. Your husband, I was told, had emigrated. Someday, I thought, I'll find out where you are and call. Maybe. My only kin, although that girl I shipped off swore she was carrying to me. How can a man be sure? Life is hard on females when they're trapped that way unless, of course, they set the trap themselves and pay the price of such deception.

The Brady girl was gone when I awoke this morning. I'll tell you about her as I go along. She'll be back shortly with my breakfast. Once or twice she's hinted about what happened that afternoon. She knows better than to refer to it openly. I still can't think about it without emotion, let alone talk about it, to her, to anyone.

—A raving beauty, the Matron, Norma Butler, described her the day I brought her in. It was Mervyn Johnston, our local fieldwarden, who first drew attention to her.

—She's in a bad way, Mister Murphy, an orphan you might say, and won't listen to me. You'll have to see her for yourself.

I went out to the townland of Drumlanna and found her sitting among the ruins of a tumbled cottage. I was startled when I saw her.

No mere flower on a dungheap. There was something

out of the ordinary about her expression and manner. At first she said no to the red ticket. I felt the glands on her neck, looked down her throat. No sign of disease. I persuaded her then to change her mind, explaining there were things I could arrange as Master that would make life more bearable. Let me be honest now and say it was the brute in me that made me so persuasive, made it hard not to stare, to imagine that body under those pitiable rags. When she said yes, I offered her a seat behind me as far as the town, told her she'd have to dismount and walk from the outskirts to the poorhouse itself. It wouldn't be seemly for the Master to be seen bringing in a female pauper on horseback. I was surprised when she refused the offer with a headshake.

—Then walk on, girl, I said.

For three miles I watched her walking, her gait graceful as that of a trained dancer. Compared with most country girls she trod the road like a racehorse. Once or twice I tried talking. Each time she pretended not to understand. Then I saw tears on her face and remembered what it was like to be deep in grief, homeless and alone in the world, as we were once, at the mercy of strangers. The rest of the journey passed in silence.

I put her to childminding in the female children's ward. When not with me in this room she sleeps on a stretcher near the oven in the bake-house. It's warm and not as sickly foul as the female dormitory or the idiot ward where her mother's lodged. She brings my meals to this room, cleans it out every day, and the pantry off, and the boardroom next door when the Board of Guardians are due to meet.

A raving beauty now seems an odd description for a girl who opens her legs more readily than she opens her mouth though, when she does speak, it's to ask pointed questions. She must have crept away quietly in the half-light this morning. Prefers not to be seen coming and going to the Master's room.

—But you bring my meals here, I said, it's part of your work.

—Not at night, she said.

I thought about this for a while.

—Is there talk?

No answer but, once, deep asleep, I heard her mutter.

—Jealous cunts.

So I woke her and asked,

—Who's jealous?

She pretended not to understand. I told her what she said, using the blunt word she'd used to startle her into response.

—And why would anyone be jealous?

—That's my question.

She responded with a shrug and a stare from those green, cat-brazen eyes. Silly to ask. Who wants me, who wants me not? Vain and silly. Clean well-water, the leftovers of fresh bread, the cuttings of cheese and meat scraps she gets from my table. That's what she wants; that's what brings her to this bed. Not me. Hunger.

When she first arrived I showed her the fifty-gallon water barrel I draw from a mountain spring near Derravarragh. Fortnightly. I told her to drink nothing else. Ever. It's a granite landscape up there. The water's like crystal with a kind of bluey tinge. I watch her drinking it from a glass, and she watches me watching with those knowing eyes. It's like being watched by a wild animal. Sometimes when I give her butter, bread and honey, she trembles while eating. A little colour comes into her face, but the manner is unafraid, insolent almost in one so young. Clearly her looks promote envy and, as you must know, girls endowed that way tend to have high notions of their worth.

She was here two full weeks before I touched her. When I did, she looked at me for what seemed like a minute or longer, until I was obliged to ask,
—Do you object?
—How can I?
—By saying no!
To this she made no answer but continued staring in silence which I read as consent. She seldom talks before, during, or after congress. More disconcerting, she utters no sound, no hint or moan of pleasure. Oddly, as I became familiar with her body the less I seemed to know her mind and began to wonder was there any mind worth knowing. Then one night out of nowhere she surprised me by asking,
—Do you have kin?
—Not that I know.
In the silence that followed I knew that reply was half true, half false.
—Are you Catholic or Protestant?
—Neither.
—You're not Christian so?
—I was baptised Catholic, I said, but expect nothing from this world or the next.
—So what made your mother put a name like Reggie on you?
I was unready for these sudden questions. Even less did I care for the blunt way they were asked.
—My kin, creed, or name is no affair of yours, girl, I said.
She was silent for a while, then shrugged faintly.
—The priest Galligan says you have a sister, married out of Granard.
—Does he now?
—He does, so he does.
—A knowing man is the Reverend Galligan! I said.

—It's what he told me.
—I'm sure he did.

Clever little thing, I thought. She knew I'd be angered by the idea of Galligan nosing into my life. Clearly he'd got word from some long-eared cleric in Longford. A holy finger in every pie, they have, and more than a finger, if truth be told, which they seldom tell but damn little they don't know about the ups and downs in towns and townlands, the streets and cities of this saintly island, and what they don't hear in confession gets whispered and altered elsewhere, at crossroads and schoolyards, in parochial parlours and sacristies.

—She bragged it herself, Father.
—True as God, your Reverence.
—Not a dog in the street but has it.
—Every ass in the bog knows it for fact.
—May I be struck dead if I'm tellin' a word of a lie.

Or maybe she heard it from Hanratty, the sub-master here, an Armagh sacristan's son, an ex-seminarian with a big head and mock priesty voice, creeping about the boys' dormitory at night, listening at doors and windows. A seminal man in league with the clergy, spying, scheming and informing. Bred in him. My Lord-ing Old Clonroy at the beginning and end of every sentence. Told me once he'd lost his vocation at Maynooth after two years.

—In bed, I asked him, or in a sheugh? Well, Ratty, I greet him each morning. How many dead? What's the count?

He pretends to enjoy black banter but loathes me, thank God. I can tell from his fixed smile and the way he never looks me in the eye. Nonetheless I'd prefer him to the priest Galligan, by a rat's whisker. It was that sly reference to your existence and to your poverty that angered me, made me snap back,

—If there is a hell there's more priests than whores in it, and I am Sir to you, girl! What else about Galligan?
—Have you mortal sins on your soul? he asked me. Is the man Murphy using you?
—Did you tell him to go to hell?
—It's bad luck to curse a priest — Sir.
—Did you tell him you were using 'the man Murphy'?
—I don't have a foodpress — Sir.
—So?
—I want to stay alive, Sir.
—Then go to the dayroom and pick oakum. You don't have to come here. What else?
—He said you were a landlord's lackey, Sir, a traitor to Ireland, and would surely burn in the lowest pit of hell.

Those words were like a stomach punch. I tried not to show how they struck home.

—That fella's a traitor to common sense, and make no mistake, girl, I'm Master here. If he lifts a finger to you or an eyebrow to me, it's out on his arse he'll go. You can tell him that if you want.

Sudden anger had made me deaf to her next question which I had to make her repeat.

—I asked you, Sir, was he lying about your sister?
—Trying to make trouble.

I then heard myself say,
—She was an infant when we were parted.

I could see her thinking behind those green eyes that looked directly into mine and began to wish she'd stayed as silent as she appeared to be when she first came here.

—That was a cruel thing they did, Sir.
—They had no choice, maybe.
—And no sight of her since? Your own sister?

I then realised this was more than country cuteness. Here was a little vixen playing off one man against another, prying deep into privacy but, worse again, playing the hypocrite and thinking I wouldn't or couldn't twig it.

—You don't visit your mother in the idiot ward, I said. She's dying, you do know that?

Her response was to look away for a moment and then find another question deliberately meant to irritate. I didn't bother answering and tried to tell myself I was in no way bothered by her. Certainly not my conscience. I've no guilt about what happens in this bed, or this room, because the more I see of death every day the more I crave congress every night. Most likely she hates me for having to come here at all, and there's something in me that dislikes her coming, but when those arms are around my neck it's like that whispering mouth in Calcutta long ago. More and more now I try to discourage it from talking but she manages most times to slip in an enquiry about passage money, knowing well I can arrange it with Clonroy. I explain each time. A 'free' five pounds steerage ticket to America could be a death warrant. Cramped, stifling, shit-filthy conditions, and wretched food would sicken a dog. She doesn't believe or only half believes me.

—What does it cost to go cabin?

—Twenty pounds, a great deal of money, and you bring your own food and water, and you need another twenty for when you get there.

—I can work for that, Sir. If you'd loan me I'll send it back.

—You want me to loan you forty pounds!

She stared at me and made no answer, so I said,

—A girl like you? Alone? In New York? Boston? Put it out of your head.

—Why?

—The dock rats'd get you for a brothel.

—I'm a hoor you think, Sir?

The Master

—They'd make you one.
—Have you not done that, Sir?
—Your choice, girl, and mind your tongue!

Next day I didn't go to the foodpress when she was drinking water. The day after that she was a track more mannerly, like a dog that sees you reaching for the cane; biddable, but not cowering.

Once, after intimacy, I heard her mutter,
—You don't own me.

I said I had no wish to own or dominate, and asked her to explain. She refused, but did say at another time,
—The Mother thought she owned us. That was her mistake.

Of course the dream they all dream is America, America, America. Paradise! Happiness! Freedom! Abundance! Meantime, the nightmare is here and now and being awake to the other bodies lodged in this house, half alive and otherwise. Who in God's name or the Devil's would want to own them? All boding time till abide with me. Yours, hers, mine, and theirs. Grave matter. That's what I'm master of. Till my time is up! Must be one of the most unenviable posts in the history of the world thus far. They called Christ 'Master' long ago but I'm a long way from Him and in sore need of a few miracles. Like all of us I'd like to ask Him some questions about man- and womankind, about why He made us and the world the way it is, and how and when He means to end it? Or why if He means to end it did He bother making it at all? And the billions of stars and beyond? What purpose? How can anyone look about the world and believe in a God? How can anyone look about the world and not believe in a God? Is it some cruel game He's playing up there? Lep at the stars and break your neck?

When I got up this morning I went to the admittance book to check when she came in. There it was in

Hanratty's elaborate hand:

February the third 1848
Brady, Roisin/Female/Age 17, RC/Not disabled/Very
clean/Townland of Drumlanna/Tenant of Eden Hall
Estate/House tumbled.

Underneath I'd scribbled,

Mother confined to idiot ward. Only kin.

Like me, one frail tie she can't wait to untie.

Last night we had to close the gates forcibly. About two dozen were locked out. Most of them slept under the canal bridge. Earlier, from the window, I could see some stirring, others still. Dead still. They'll be carted later to the open pit behind the turfshed along with the ones found in ditches and sheughs and the poor wretches the Council fish out of the canal from time to time, all of them consigned to perpetual light or darkness with their neighbours from a hundred townlands. Galway and Scarriff have just been closed by the treasury. Overspending, they say, and every pauper who could walk was shown the road to everlasting. This place has become a kind of Public School for the impoverished. Their only lesson? How to die, and I am death's headmaster. Soon we'll have to open another pit. Most masters don't like using paupers for the pit digging. I never had qualms that way until recently. Hired labour, being costly, meant less money to buy food and every circular from the Castle used the word 'rationalise' at least three times. It was the priest Galligan who protested,
—Unseemly, he said, to have the dead burying the dead.
I shrugged him off by saying,

The Master

—Kings or paupers, I said, we all dispose of each other, this way, when the time comes. And priests? Does it matter how?

I could see him looking with disbelief.

But I must tell you that many things I considered ridiculous then now appear to me in a very different and painful light. Certainly I'll ask for voluntary teams to do the digging from now on, if I decide to stay on.

Did I tell you that, a month back in the Phoenix Park, the Viceroy looked at me and asked,

—Who are you, Sir?

I told him but thought to myself, who in hell is he? For that matter who is anybody, in heaven or in hell? When our parents christened me Lonan Reginald Murphy in Calcutta they'd no notion I'd say of calling me Reggie which I quickly became, for obvious reasons. Clonroy's name is Bob Skinner and the Viceroy who laid the first stone at Maynooth was a man called Pratt. More fitting, we now have an English ex-general in charge of Poor Law relief, food for the starving, and he's called Sir Edward Pine Coffin! A decent man they say but the Dickens of a name, with quarter of a million in poorhouses, up on three millions or more starving and Christ knows how many wandering the roads or packed into coffin ships, one in five dumped at sea. I've a thousand in this place built for six hundred. None of them can afford a shroud let alone a coffin.

> *Rattle my bones over the stones,*
> *I'm a poor pauper nobody owns.*
> *Where am I going, where am I bound?*
> *Naked and lonely into the ground.*

No, sister, I'm not being cynical. I'm trying to be candid about brutal facts. As Master here I admit paupers. That's my work. From entry to exit, public ward to burial pit. Eighty-seven last week. Lurgan was unluckier; they had ninety-eight. It's what we Masters are paid for, processing paupers, and better paid than a postmaster or station-master, but they don't have to traffic with dysentery, cholera, typhus, or be present when we sign in families and then segregate them, husband from wife, parents from children, or listen to the crying and keening I'd almost ceased to hear, the way people who live near rookeries no longer hear the rooks. But I do see a lot of them go mad with grief which I now understand in a deeper way.

In truth I'm cangled to grief for fifty pounds a year and it's not enough. Six of us, workhouse Masters that is, died this past twelve months, along with nine priests, two chaplains, seven doctors, all in the line of duty. Typhus mostly. They haven't a pup's notion how it spreads.

I know. In fact I'm certain. It's the water contaminated by corpses. You can smell it. Yes, it is a dangerous occupation, but I've emigrated dead paupers from time to time and collected a small bonus for the extra bookwork involved! Nothing criminal, you must understand. I'm trying to be candid. I'm no saint, sister, as you'll have gathered, but I'm far from the worst which would leave me about the same as the rest of man- and womankind.

Yesterday two weeks back was Saint Patrick's feast day. It came in mild. Galligan said Mass in the men's yard with my permission. Segregation was strictly enforced, as always. Chaos otherwise, mothers with suckling infants excepted, though mostly they're suckling at nothing. All trooping out to kneel like ghosts in the March sunlight. Afterwards two paupers with a tin whistle and a squeezebox wheezed out a few melodies, Tom Moore's weepy parlour stuff, dreams that never were, nor ever will be. Then all sang feebly, Galligan leading loudly,

The Master

 —Hail glorious, Saint Patrick, dear saint of our isle,
 On us, thy poor children, bestow a sweet smile.

Stringer, our chaplain, kept his poor Protestants apart in the main hall, hymning their way to heaven. Wilson's bakery donated a thousand sweet fingers to mark the day. One each at noon. Amid the fast a pauper's feast. Fingers of death. Three died during Mass. The ablebodied carried them away to the dead cart and eternity.

If you think the conveying of these details a little cold let me give you an item or two from my Complaints Book. Here's the kind of thing I've had to write up again and again:

COMPLAINT

The Roman Catholic priest, Brendan Galligan, objects forcefully to the Church of Ireland chaplain, Norman Stringer, deliberately reading the Bible in the school house with Papist children present.

MASTER'S RULING

Catholic children to be removed during Bible readings.

COMPLAINT

The Protestant chaplain, Norman Stringer, protests angrily that the priest Galligan brings in and distributes 'bagfulls of rosaries, medals, trinkets and other such trumpery to Protestant children during school hours'.

MASTER'S RULING

The priest Galligan must desist from this practice.

And these fellows call themselves apostles of Christ. Holy men? Holy God, Holy hell! Stupid, stupid, stupid men! And I'm obliged to nod to both but you'll pardon me, sister, when I tell you that I fart as I nod, when possible, because I don't give a pauper's shite about the breed or creed of either. I'm fairly sure they see me as evil but, God knows, I'm nowhere near as devious as such masters of promise and pretence.

The Brady girl came back with my breakfast as I began to set down this confession. I ate a little without appetite, gave her some bread and a decent hunk of cheese from the foodpress. She looked at me with something close to disbelief, ate both quickly and gulped down two glasses of water. She then muttered thank you so quietly it might have been a curse. As she left the Kilkenny dream came back with sudden clarity. I was in that middle classroom in the catacombs of St Paul's, as old Darling barked out his obsession with words:

—*Phytophthora infestans*?

—Come on, boys. *Phytophthora infestans*, Murphy? What does it mean?

—I don't know, Sir.

—With a name like yours! *Phytophthora infestans* is a blight, Murphy, and here in Ireland at the peak of our Empire it has brought famine, poverty and death on a scale more harrowing than the worst areas of Calcutta. This island, always a backdoor nuisance to the greater island, is now a scarecrow in a foul rickyard, a rotting corpse in an empty larder caused, you must surely know, by the arrival of this blight, this disease of the common spud or Murphies. The word itself derives from the Anglo-Saxon *blican*, a lightning strike, or possibly from the Middle German *blichen*, to grow pale, to decay, to die. Thus the word has become synonymous with, Murphy? With?

—Death, Sir!

Like most dreams, illogical nonsense. Famine? How could it be? In a country exporting food on every tide? Certainly there was no blight, famine or starvation when

The Master

I was at St Paul's apart from the blight of loneliness. They allowed me out for Instruction and Confession every Saturday.

On Sundays I went to Mass in the town, emancipated! We were all emancipated by then, we Irish Roman Catholics. Whatever army benefit there was went on my schooling. You got nothing, Annie, but the coach fare from Cobh to Granard and a midland bog. Sometimes I envied the remoteness of a life like that. I was a curiosity. Being the only Papist was a challenge to bullies, three in particular who couldn't leave me be.

—Tell us, Spud, is it true you Papes believe Jesus Christ is in a wafer, blood and bone?

I held my tongue.

—Do you eat him guts and all?

I held my tongue.

—Do rascally priests feel you people up at Confession?

I held my tongue.

—Did *your* man ever try that on you?

At which I blurted,

—You silly shits, go bugger each other!

They tackled me then but I was strong, still am, and not being gentle born I fought back with teeth, boots, and nails. Two of them were bruised and scrabbed, the third badly enough bitten for the infirmary. They never tackled me again, even though I'd mutter 'Silly shits' any time they were near.

It was during that first Christmas holiday I realised my reports were sent both to Eden Hall and Derrylester. Old Clonroy sent for me. When I arrived I could see he had a copy of my report, and if his face was serious his manner was benign.

—Under *Conduct and Behaviour* it says here, 'Inclined to brutal tactics. Unprovoked. One boy treated in the infirmary. Two others badly marked. Recurrence may mean expulsion.' This has your headmaster's signature. What was it about, boy?

—My religion, my Lord, was being mocked.

—Not worth fighting over, he said. Most religion is make-believe, most mockery envy. You should have ignored both.

When I'd finished at Kilkenny, he sent for me again.

—So! You've started well. Not the top, but close enough. Very good. But what are we going to do with you now, eh? Soldiering? Like your father? Best regiments in the world are Irish. It's one thing we're damned good at here, fighting! No? Law? I could get you apprenticed. No? Then you tell me what's in your head.

I said I loved Derrylester, house and farm. I'd become attached to the Fergusons and I liked farming.

—The idea of it, perhaps. Farming, he went on to say, was hard enough at the best of times. Hereabouts with our Irish hackers and poisoners it can be a bloody nightmare, fortress farming, and don't forget we're all slightly mad in this country. Inbreeding mostly, and religious nonsense.

The kettle calling the pot black. Dust and disorder seemed more offensive to him than death. Last time he was here he barked out,

—When were those windows cleaned, Murphy? A new building and you can hardly see through the windows! Surely you can delegate some paupers for the job.

Most paupers, I explained, were too weak to climb ladders, let alone clean windows.

Barracks life since he was twenty, all that marching and killing for Queen and Empire has him half crazy like most old soldiers. Unpolished boots more likely to keep him wakeful than some poor sapper's death. Or paupers. Nor did I like to suggest that as a farmer I'd be viewed differently from the titled descendant of a Cromwellian

The Master

settler with twenty thousand acres of confiscated land. Derrylester was a modest holding not likely to inspire the envy or hatred that seemed to cling like arrogance or a bad odour to the owners of big estates. Nor did I want to tell him what old Sam Ferguson had said to me once, his eyes full of tears,

—You're more to me than a son, you must know that.

I do know he meant it. There were a hundred freehold acres at Derrylester of well fenced, well laid-out fields, a sound, cut stone house, yards and barns, an orchard garden, half a mile of trout river, a ten-acre lake, an artesian well eighty feet deep in the flagged dairy and a herd of fifty shorthorn cattle, roans, reds and blues, that took prizes for milk and beef wherever they were shown. It was near paradise, to my mind.

Naturally I stayed on and worked as an unpaid steward, eighteen years of hard work, the neverending watch for thieving and idling of tenant workers, and dairymaids! They could be lively but I wasn't free for that kind of freedom. I had to be circumspect about how I paid myself and about private matters. Still have to be. Along with the mixed farming we kept a hunt pack. Fallen animals for miles about were dumped in the yard to feed hounds. Dear God, that deathly smell of bloated beasts in high summer. Even in winter it lingered in my clothes and hair, a mix of dogshit, entrails and rotting flesh.

Every now and then a plague of rats had to be poisoned. No one would or could flay those carcasses but me. The old man was too arthritic so I accustomed my stomach to the fact and smell of animal death. What made others retch instantly was nothing to me, the perfect apprenticeship for my work as Master of this poorhouse, workhouse, union, call it what you like. What's in a name?

A great deal, I was soon to learn. Too late. The old man's nephew, Richard, wrote from Australia once a year. He had no other kin. I was shown the letters, no sense of a special bond, but Sam replied. Naturally I didn't see his replies but hoped, presumed, I was to inherit. Meantime, in truth, I liked the work, and I loved the place, and so stayed on happily enough.

I can narrow down my love for that farm to one day, and one field, the lake meadow, with its great single beech in the middle. During that midsummer's day under a glorious sun with ten Fermanagh men, I scythed down a hundred and fifty rucks. There was still light when we quit the field near midnight. Two rainless weeks later it was stacked and thatched in the haggard and, because engendering is proscribed in heaven, the smell of green hay, I remember thinking, must be what they use up there to engender happiness. Some day, I imagined, I'd be master of the earth, water and sky over Derrylester, without the snarling of dogs or the odour of dead animals, mowing grass under a summer sun or feeding green scented hay in midwinter, till kingdom come.

It was not to be. When he died, the house and garden were willed to the old lady for her lifetime and, thereafter, everything — land, lock, stock and barrel — to his nephew, Richard.

I couldn't think or speak for days. They thought I was heartbroken about the old man passing on. Gradually I began to understand. Blood goes deep. It tells. And names do matter. Ours, Murphy, is like a brand here in Ulster, and even though I was moulded and educated to their likeness I was bred from the conquered tribe. Stupidly I'd ignored what I'd heard them mulling over in their hot whiskies.

—Aye, you can rear the wild thing, Sam, and ye think ye know it, but some day it'll growl and tear your throat out! The identical same with Taigs. Keep an eye, keep your distance, keep them out.

That, I knew, was an article of faith with the more ignorant type of Presbyterian and, while I was certain old Ferguson was not such a one, I should have realised I wasn't blood. Like it or not, I was a Taig.

In his will he referred to my 'good education and good head to use it. He will better himself in the world. I have no doubt of this. I leave him three hundred guineas and, as a token of my special affection, the silver embossed snuff box willed me by my father, Alex.'

Not mean, but to buy and stock even a modest farm it was less than a pittance. My life was half gone. I'd bided my time for a dream, for nothing. I almost kicked the snuff box into a boghole, changed my mind and pawned it at Enniskillen for one guinea and, fond as I was of old Hannah Ferguson, I left suddenly. Since then I expect nothing from anyone, take what's my due and more if it's safe. The thing nearest to my heart was suddenly gone, like our mother and father, in thirteen words. It was like death again: 'To my nephew, Richard Ferguson, I leave the farmlands and house at Derrylester.'

I heard nothing further as the attorney droned on, itemising bequests. So names do matter, blood does tell, and some hurts never heal.

That disappointment clenched my heart against expectation of any kind and a heart clenched, Annie, becomes a cold thing. It has to. It would seem now that I am rummaging about for excuses, for exoneration. Whether or not, I am trying to be candid and most abjectly begging your forgiveness. In truth these past few years I've become unkind, not just dead to feeling, unkind. It was, I decided, the only way to function in this world. Never again would I allow life to betray me as it had. To hurt me. You will think now, sister, that I'm straying far from you in this account. Let me beg your patience a little longer while I tell you why I agreed to become Master of this place, what that means, and how that must affect and alter, not only me, but any man in my position. Or woman. Above all, why I greeted you as I did.

That hard blow, the will, came sometime late in March of 1843. At Eden Hall they'd heard about it and my sudden leavetaking. Old Clonroy sent for me. He was as I always found him, oblique, kindly, and a little odd. I thought he was referring indirectly to the will when he said,

—You'll find life a lot easier without expectations of any kind.

Two years later, when Eden Hall went on the market, I realised he was thinking about himself when he said that, being the last of the line and betrayed in a way by kin, his only son, Mathew. Three hundred years of continuity discontinued, but all of that's another story. Why he sent for me was to tell me that his neighbour and friend, Mr Shirley, a direct descendant of the Earl of Essex and owner of Castle Fea, a whole barony of south Monaghan which ran to near seventy thousand acres, had just engaged a new land agent, an Englishman called Stuart Trench. Would I care to act as sub-agent and translator?

The money offered was tempting. It had to be. It was a time when landlords and their agents were being assassinated or half beaten to death all over Ireland. I didn't want the job but without training for other work I was in no position to refuse. Three days later, April the third, I found myself alongside Trench outside the agent's house in the main street of Carrickmacross. He was only a week in the country but I'd been with him for three days, got to know him a little. I liked him, though I kept wanting to stop him and say, 'It's not England here, Sir, nor Scotland, nor Wales. It's as different as France or Spain.' He was listening, not hearing, but being a clever man I felt he'd learn quickly.

That morning outside the agent's house he was standing on a table to make sure he could be heard, and a commanding voice and manner he had; very sure of himself. I was on a chair beside him to interpret for that south Monaghan crowd, a huge, ragged mass of hungry humans as far as we could see, and a cold, hasky day it was. Showers of sleet and rain. There was something in excess of ten thousand, the Constabulary said afterwards.

What I had to convey from Trench speaking for his new master was bad news. There was, I had to shout out, a vast amount of rent owing. The estate was in real danger of bankruptcy. There could be no question whatsoever of forgoing or reducing rent. He also talked of 'appropriate action in the event of non-payment' which I could only translate as 'bad news for the house', a euphemism for eviction. This went through the crowd like a growl, followed by a deathly silence, till a voice shouted out in both tongues,

—Down on your knees, boys, we'll ask him again on our knees.

And that huge crowd were suddenly bareheaded on their knees in a silence so absolute you could hear the daws racketing in the town chimneys. I had seen the kneeling before and knew it to be a form of abjection both sinister and threatening. Trench was startled.

—What's going on? he asked through the side of his mouth.

—What you see, I whispered. Abject supplication.

I could tell he was more irritated than afraid or, if afraid, he didn't show it. He seemed almost unaware of the menace.

—Any suggestions?
—I'd promise them something.

Maybe it was the urgency of my whisper that made

him say aloud,

—I'm damned if I will!

Was that sidemouth whisper overheard? Or was it Trench's unafraid mutter and shrug? I don't know but suddenly, without warning, the table upended, he was grabbed and disappeared. There followed a frenzy of milling and shouting so turbulent, so enraged and hysterical, that I couldn't see him being stripped, punched, beaten and kicked, because he didn't call out.

I knew roughly where he was and was trying to get to him when suddenly I saw him, almost naked and upright, both arms pinned against a cartwheel, a crowd of men round him with cudgels, screeching into his face in a language that needed no interpreter.

I don't think I've ever been so frightened in my life, not so much for myself as for what I feared was about to happen. Maybe it was sudden fear that gave me the strength to jostle my way towards him, shouting out,

—The man's new. Give him a chance. Don't, men, don't. He's a stranger!

Or it might have been when I shouted out,

—For Jesus' sake, don't murder the man, lads, don't do it, they'll hang you!

Maybe it was the words 'murder' and 'hang' that caused a lull because suddenly I was at his side and he had voice and courage enough to shout out,

—I will do everything in my power to persuade Mister Shirley of the strength of your feelings and ask him to reconsider the justice of your case.

This I translated as,

—Listen, lads, he knows your troubles, but he needs your patience and good nature to sort things out. Will ye give the man a chance?

At which some voice shouted out,

—God bless you, Stuart Trench.

The Master

And as quick as the kneeling crowd turned ugly the standing crowd now began to cheer and shout down blessings on his head.

I worked with Trench for a learning year. He was still arrogant but a great deal more circumspect. He convinced Mister Shirley that emigrating tenant paupers to America at five pounds a head was cheaper than keeping them in the poorhouse at four pounds a year. By buying passage he'd be free of the swarming cottiers, squatters and ditch beggars who couldn't pay rent and were, in any case, half starving because of the blight. He would benefit, they would benefit. The scheme was a huge success till the black tide of sea burials came floating back to haunt every family in the country.

Meantime Lord Lansdowne had heard of the scheme and written Shirley. Could he recommend someone to emigrate three thousand tenants from his estate in Kenmare in the County of Kerry? I was approached and said why not. I knew the system, the pay was better, the climate milder, the people more colourful than the dour tidy Scots-English I'd grown up amongst, and they were clamouring for tickets. So down I went, and for two years bank drafts of four hundred pounds arrived regularly. I shipped between two and three hundred tenants a week from Kenmare to Queenstown on foot. It was like an ancient cattle drive but not as easy. The road was filled with men, women and children, singing and laughing, clowning and arguing along with their pigs, goats, fowl, donkeys, creels and carts, all of them elated and heartbroken because this was a farewell forever to the garden of spuds, to hearth and hovel, to mountain and bog, to Mother Ireland herself. So they all kept shouting up in tears and waving to the poor scarecrows hoeing in turnip fields.

—We're on our way to Amerikay!

And the poor scarecrows would wave back. The dead waving farewell to the dead.

If the weather was against us we'd have to overnight. That was always trouble. The appetite for porter being insatiable leads on to fighting and shouting and wandering and no end of rounding up. With only three paid henchmen this caused serious delays. Unlike Ulster folk, these Kerry people were without a word of English. Most of them had never been more than a mile or so outside their own townlands. They were the same people Saint Patrick had preached to in the fifth century, noisy, good humoured, unpredictable, and the young ones now far from the prying eyes of neighbours were none too particular about their conduct, much of which I could see from horseback. In their own heads, I suppose, they were bound for the excitements of another world, a great adventure, not knowing that one in five would indeed end up in another world, ocean deep.

Last year, of the two-hundred-and-twenty thousand emigrated, forty thousand died on the way or on arrival. It was nothing like that when I was down there but I became uneasy as newspapers began writing of 'Extermination', 'Bloodletting', and 'Innocents consigned to the deep', and described me as 'An Ulster turncoat, the cruel whipmaster of Lansdowne's death riders'. So you will understand that when a letter came from Eden Hall telling me about a new workhouse on the outskirts of the town I moved quickly. Being Master of a workhouse up here seemed both safer and more attractive than being a death rider in Kerry. I knew also that the position itself tends to inspire a kind of awe akin to gentry or clergy.

I have to confess that I wasn't indifferent to that. Also, I was glad to be back in my own province where I'd once been happy at Derrylester although, any time I passed it,

The Master

I could see slates missing and great patches of nettles flowering in the orchard garden. Hannah Ferguson had died when I was away and the land, now rented out to cattle dealers and jobbers, was already reverting to ragwort and rushes.

Have I already told you that some time in February of this year the Viceroy, Clarendon, requested a delegation of a dozen masters, three from each province, to discuss the increased death rate in almost all of the hundred-and-fifty poorhouses? I travelled up with John Wynne of Carrickmacross who was very much in the news at the time. At some point I said the workhouse system itself was causing the increase. Clarendon had already asked my name but glanced down at his notes to make sure.

—Mister Murphy? You're not serious?

—I'm certain, I said. It's putrefaction from burial pits leaking into workhouse wells, infecting staff and paupers. Our pit's at the march of our twelve acres but I wouldn't drink the water.

—Your paupers drink it?

—They have no choice, nor have we. With a thousand souls, we must pump water.

—What solution would you suggest, Sir?

—I'd burn the corpses.

This caused quite a silence till John Wynne said,

—My Lord, I'm inclined to agree with Mister Murphy. Cremation is a more cleansing process, my Lord.

Clarendon knew John Wynne. A while back some peeping squint of a squireen had seen him 'at it' in a ditch with a pauper girl and written to Dublin Castle about the shock this vision had caused to what he called his 'moral sensibility'. All hell then broke over Wynne's head. He was the Devil incarnate using his position to seduce poor dying pauper girls. The poor girls were dying to seduce him for anything going, extra food rations, passage money, or shenanigans for the sake of shenanigans.

I know. He ended up in the House of Lords defending himself and was acquitted, but then they'd respond well to him over there. He's a bit craven about position and titles, My Lord-ing Clarendon at the beginning and end of every sentence, and Clarendon is a very Patrician gentleman, but he farts, shits and copulates like any other man and he's afraid of the Catholic Church.

—The Church of Rome, he said, will not discuss cremation. I will not antagonise them. We have more than enough on our hands, gentlemen.

—But when families die of typhus, I said, the hovel's burned over them and the clergy sprinkle ashes. That's cremation surely? Why pretend it's not?

—I cannot answer for the Church of Rome, Clarendon muttered.

To which I almost added, An institution run by hypocrites for idiots.

I held my tongue but let me say now that, as a practising hypocrite, I'm moderately gifted. My position here obliges me to give out morning and evening prayers and grace before meals.

—Bless us, O Lord, and these Thy gifts which of Thy bounty we are about to receive.

If I had my way I'd consign most holy men to the idiot wards but then the paupers would be desolate. They cling to them, hang on every word. Heaven's next door, over the hill, upstairs, round the corner, destination of the destitute. Naked, diseased, raving, filthy and skeletal, they go straight to the arms of Jesus and Mary! It's alms we need from Jesus and Mary to clothe the naked and feed the hungry.

—The poor you have always with you. Me you have not.

Quare big notions You had of Yourself. Jesus, God of

love. Small wonder they crucified You!

Annie, I'm sorry if such notions offend you, but anger, as you made so clear to me, is a comrade to grief and all day I've been penning this confession to explain both. I've been to the press just now and poured the tumbler of whiskey that numbs before it worsens. Twice during the day the Brady girl has tapped on the door asking if I wanted to eat in the staff room or here. I've no appetite whatever and tell her what I've been telling her every day, that I'm still unwell, but on the mend. Not true. Time may be a healer for the body. For the soul, in my case, it's no cure. In truth, to my mind, it can sicken even more.

It's dusk now, near dark again, and there's the Angelus ringing high over the clatter and murmur coming up from the paupers' dining hall. Somewhere — it must be from the female sleeping quarters — I can hear an infant crying and crying and crying and it wrings my heart. I don't know why. Or perhaps I do because every hour of this long day I've been aware of the coming night, the night of ending. The night of Lady's Day.

Let me tell you that from daybreak it's threatened rain from a sky as black as the Bangor blues on the roof of the admissions block. It held off somehow, and somehow I've been holding out against that word 'admissions', much like the children's game where 'yes' or 'no' is the forbidden word but no child ever wins. Nor can I when that word comes into my head.

I'll pour another tumbler and tonight, instead of evicting memory, I'll try to explain. And there's another word, explain, explain, explain! How many times have I used it when in my heart of hearts I know there is no explanation that deserves forgiveness? None. But I have tried to grapple with some few details of what we call life with all the honesty I can muster, and maybe that deserves a morsel of mitigation. Does it not? Bless me, Mother, Father, Creator, Lord Jesus, Allah, Buddah, Somebody, Nobody, Anybody. Bless me, bless me, bless me, for I have sinned and am sorrowful. My sister, Annie, bless me and forgive me. Can you hear me? I am talking to you and no one else and let me not grow mawkish nor evasive when the whiskey throngs, nor unafraid to admit right off that soft-sounding word 'admissions', nor to tell you what it signifies. Let me say it aloud,

—Admissions.

Workhouse admissions. Work. Not pleasant but it becomes routine like all work. Families mostly, starving of course, must agree to sign over all rights to land and property. Before we can admit them they must prove destitution, and then walk away forever from neighbour and village, field and well, hearth and home.

We supply the documents proving poverty. They line up and I question them. Name, townland, religion, landlord, and so on. Then I make sure they understand that the house they have just left will be tumbled, levelled back into the landscape. Mostly they're too weak and sick to take this in. A clerk writes down details. They make their mark. I sign them in and pass them on to the medical officer, O'Grady.

The doctor before him, Ambrose O'Donnell, was hopeless. We all agreed about that. He was either in, or on the edge of, tears most of the time. And a big strong Donegal fella he was. Caused great upset. He couldn't stomach the process and had to go. As he was leaving he told me he'd rather be a pauper than an admitting officer and I remember thinking at the time, this man is quite mad; certainly he's weak, foolish, unbalanced. I now think the very opposite.

When the physical condition is decided by O'Grady, segregation takes place. Men, women, boys, girls, proceed to separate quarters where they remain separate till they sign out, which is, in many cases, lights out. It can be noisy. The orderlies, most of them able-bodied paupers, are there to protect me and the admitting staff from outlandish behaviour, hysterical kneeling, shrieking and begging, the throwing of arms around our legs.

Hanratty's good at calming them and the Matron, Norma Butler. They take them aside and talk quietly. If they're unhappy about segregation, then they're free to go. There's no obligation to come in. They have of course nowhere to go so they say their goodbyes and are led to the washhouses and from there to the dayrooms, workrooms, yards, schoolhouse, fever shed, idiot ward, or often straight to the dying rooms where, during this last year, they mostly end.

That morning of the twenty-fifth of March, admissions were going quietly. Generally they're so desolate they've no energy for making scenes, but halfway down the line I noticed a woman, wild-eyed and standing out. She was holding a child by the hand, both emaciated, the child in a bag skirt wearing a man's cap so I couldn't tell its gender.

She was looking at me very directly. I kept avoiding her eyes but I could sense them staring in that way you can and thought, do I know her maybe from somewhere? Maybe even slept with her long ago, back in the Derrylester days? No. Surely I'd remember that. But she was familiar in some way. I knew I knew her and was thinking this when she broke line and began walking towards me dragging the child and ignoring the orderly who seemed unsure about what to do. As she approached she called out in a kind of broken voice,

—Lolo!

Oh Christ of Calcutta, that one word, a pet name from long ago, should be like a sword twist in the bowels, an invisible bullet to stop my heart like nothing I'd ever known. My breathing shallowed and I suppose my mouth fell open. She called again louder,

—Lolo!

Only one person in the world knew that pet name. As a little one, Annie, you couldn't get your mouth round my first name, Lonan, so beyond all doubt the frightened, haggard, approaching face I knew was yours, beyond doubt, and the child staring up from familiar eyes was, recognisably, my nephew, or niece. The orderly was watching me for a sign. Unnerved, I looked away to the clerk's ledger and said what I say to every pauper,

—Name?

To which she said again,

—Lolo, it's me, Annie.

—Townland?

—Your sister, Annie, Anne Marie, remember! Look at me, Lolo!

I was aware I'd lost control, could sense a curious silence, staff and paupers watching to see what would happen next.

My eyes were filling but I kept staring at the ledger, stupidly. Then I heard you shouting as though in a dream,

—For Jesus' sake, Lolo, look at me, you're my brother! I'm your sister!

I should have said something loving and familial but what came out of my mouth, may God forgive me, was,

—All female paupers are my sisters. Take your place in the line.

I glanced from the ledger to your face and saw the disbelief in your eyes as you twisted away with a kind of wail, wrenching the child after you and heading for the main gates, half running, half stumbling, stopping once briefly to gulp out curses. A lot of them I only half heard,

The Master

but I did hear clearly,

—Brother bollocks, landlords' lickarse. May the Devil blight your prick and God send you and your childer, and theirs, to rot in leperland!

They taught you to curse well down in Granard. As they echoed and re-echoed round the yard I was thinking I couldn't admit you to the squalor of a pauper's ward, separate you from your child. That was unthinkable! Into my room, or get you a cabin somewhere? Perhaps. I don't know. I'm not sure what went through my head but I knew I'd rejected you, and now you ask me why? Embarrassment and sudden anger at being trapped? Exposed? Caught off guard as you shouted out 'brother' like that, using your sex to gain advantage? A breed of blackmail? But these thoughts I knew were poor cover for the guilt that was shortly to overwhelm me, and still does.

I am not poor but I'd refused a sibling help and shelter, lest my position as Master be called into question, when in truth I'm as crooked and partial as any man. Somewhere in that clenched heart I knew as you stumbled away that I'd made the mistake of a lifetime. I wanted to shout after you but had no voice, wanted to follow but my legs were trembly, and anyway I saw the priest Galligan running to stop you, his buttocks wobbling, and even through my chaos of mind I saw that his arse wobbled in much the same way as his jowls when he talked. When he'd caught up with you at the entrance gates I'd found my voice and said to the clerk and orderlies,

—Continue admitting.

As though nothing had happened!

But I could see you at the gates with Galligan, shaking your head and wiping away tears, and then suddenly you were gone and Galligan was walking back. I watched him approaching with a kind of cold anger. I'd never before seen him chase a pauper family. Why mine? He was trespassing. He came very close to my ear and whispered,

—I tried my best. All she would say was, I'll trouble him no more.

To which I said,

—Thank you, Sir. I'll find her and mind her when we're finished here.

He stared at me for a long moment. I returned his stare till he nodded and joined the rest of the staff.

Admissions complete, I told a pauper orderly to saddle my horse but I began with a mistake no countryman should ever make when stock go missing. Instead of looking near and close I went far and wide, away down the south road to where I thought you'd be heading for. Granard. No sign. I lost hours. It was near dark when I got back, lights in the dormer windows, the heavy gates of the workhouse closed.

Something unseen, something more than dread began circling round me as I started out to look again, this time closer. How, tell me, do you find starvelings in the starving dark? So many places to look for locked out paupers. I tried them all, under the canal bridge, the eaves of the canal stores, the eaves of the butteryard, the hollow of the round tower, the Norman fort, the old graveyard with its table tombs which gave some shelter. I searched them all, calling aloud, the echo of your name coming back from long ago. Annie, Annie, Annie. I had no name for your child and said to myself that night,

—I'll find them tomorrow.

And, as I said this, the circling thing crept into my soul and I knew with certainty that you and your child were dead and that I had let ye die.

How can we know such things beforehand? Not fear, merely, or dread, but *know*. When the knock came at daybreak it was Hanratty wearing his most lugubrious face and manner. Before he spoke I said,

—Just tell me where they were found.

He did. I got through that day somehow. Cassidy, the town undertaker, said,

—They'd be best boxed together.

I agreed. Your child was a boy. I buried you according to the rite of the Catholic Church of which I am a lost member, Father Brendan Galligan officiating. Not knowing your married name nor the name for your boy he asked me what I thought about Patrick as a name.

—None better, I said, and I have to say now that his few words about 'Annie and Patrick' being 'at one in life, death, and now finally at peace, thanks be to God' filled me with a grief I had not thought possible. Like drowning, I imagine. Let me admit, confess, in addition, that he was genuinely kind. Everyone, staff, paupers, townspeople, all kindly, kinder than I deserve. I began to see, to understand as never before that we are all kin, all of a kind, all humankind. Too late.

Maybe when the heart's unkind as mine is we make enemies where we long for friends. Worst of all, I'd closed the door on my own, had missed your life and, stupidly, your death. That night I joined the chorus of grieving paupers in this place and for the first time in thirty years howled like a dog, sobbed, wept, got lost in grief, and when that was done I found I was looking at what I'd become.

Things in life I'd shrugged off as nothing now seemed monstrous. I was the Devil manifest, my soul leprous, and, leaving God aside where he lives in silence, I knew I'd have to suffer before I could forgive myself. I began to see clearly that I was trained to be alien amongst my own people. No excuses any more. I would have to make reparation.

Eugene McCabe

Two days ago I asked the porter to bring me the rags of a dead pauper. I have them here in a cupboard. They smell. I asked for them because my first instinct was to lay aside the clothes of authority and whatever I possess, put on the discards of the poor, and walk to Granard and enter the poorhouse there, as a pauper. Every night I decide on this. Every morning I decide otherwise.

Too easy, in any case. I have been Master here for three years and here I must admit myself under Hanratty, as Master. That would be fitting. That would be punishment. That word again, 'admit', like a knife.

And now it all comes flowing back. Oh God, let me not think on how they ended. The hurt and loneliness. When I saw you, Annie, you lay in death like a curled forefinger. Cradling your dead child. Thumb into forefinger. Thus.

Oh Mama, Dada, why did you leave us? Oh my poor sister, my poor people, forgive me, and may God almighty forgive me. Jesus, mercy; Mary, help.

The Landlord

31 March 1848

Bonaparte. The Tuileries. Grandiose Imperial desk. Hardly a glance:
 —Who are you?
 —General Lord Clonroy.
 —Where's the title from?
 —It's a blend of Irish and French, Sire. My grandmother was French.
 —Meaning what?
 —The king's meadow.
 —And your seat?
 —Fermanagh. South Ulster.
 —Ah!
 —At one time I was the youngest General in the English Army.
 —Serving where?
 —India. With Field Marshal Gough.
 —The Limerick clown?
 —And with the other Irish *clown*. At Waterloo!
That made him look up, the astonishing eyes full of sullen anger. I returned the stare till he muttered,
 —You didn't win.
 —On the contrary, we did.
 —Wellington's hated by his peers and public. I'm still adored. Will be till history ends.

He then stood, turned his back, lifted a haunch and farted like a schoolboy.

Is there no antidote for this dreaming nonsense? A petty landlord from Corsica makes himself 'Emperor'! Farts in my face. 'Adored'? Sees himself as a God. Like the Caesars? Dream or no dream I called him 'Sire'. Shameful.

2 April 1848

Murphy still locked in his room. The Brady girl says he eats almost nothing. Tried talking through the door. Sounds unbalanced. Muttered about entering the poorhouse as a pauper. I pretended not to hear that. Told him I'd have behaved as he did, with firmness and courtesy. How else could he have guessed she was his sister, being a child herself when he saw her last? They say she screeched, ballyragged, cursed, and left in a great huff because he asked her to stay in line. Terrible the way she was found with her child next morning. Deeply grieved since then.

Close to a fortnight now. Mourning out of all proportion. As Master for two years now how many has he buried? Thought he'd be impervious to the empire of death.

3 April 1848

Post brought a circular from Leslie. Odd fellow. Suspect crowd politically. Every way. Mad dogs or crazy dons? High Church or atheist? More books than cattle in their keep. Our crowd military and pastoral. Did nothing about it at the time. Is that as suspect? Not much I could do.

The Landlord

Castle Leslie,
 Glaslough,
  Co Monaghan
   31 March 1848

Open letter to all the considerable landowners in the Baronies of South Ulster

This morning we were wakened by a voice crying out 'Mercy, mercy, mercy', followed by keening on the front lawn. The workhouse at Kilnaleck, closed for lack of funds, leaving a straggle of paupers with nowhere to go. They arrived here before dawn, starving, cold and wretched beyond description. When we looked down the men were kneeling, the women and children standing or lying; amongst them, a young girl holding a dead infant towards our window.

Some of you may have read Carlyle's piece:
—Ireland is like a half-starved rat that crosses the path of an elephant. What must the elephant do? Squelch it, by heavens, squelch it!

We are long accustomed to being called 'The idiot daughter' by the other Island, but what creature other than a preachy, servile Scot could pen such a sentence, at such a time? It is now clear that Westminster will continue to cut funding. Our absentees don't know or care, so those of us who reside must act now. Here at Glaslough we have been using a mix of boiled turnips and India meal for hungry tenants, beggars and stray paupers. It is not appetising but is sustaining.

I know all the objections but common humanity and selfish interest suggest that common sense must be laid aside until this crisis is over. If we allow the poorest of the poor to die on our doorsteps we will never be forgiven. The result will be a death knell for the landed class, not

just here in South Ulster, but all over Ireland.
—Leslie

P.S. Heard Mathew was over at Gilmartin's. Our giddy girls say he's 'the most breathtaking creature' they've ever laid eyes on! Is he still with you? Still mad Republican? And how are you both? The above is doomsday rhetoric but I believe it. It's an age since we've seen either your good self or 'Poor Knoggins'. We must rectify that soon.

It was Leslie first called her 'Poor Knoggins'. Ironic clownerie that stuck. She rather likes it. Showed her the above after dinner. Watched her read. Affected by paupers crying out and dead infant. Then asked,
—How many is he talking about? Hundreds? Thousands? Strolling or lying about on our front lawn? Drinking raw poteen? Where will they shelter? In our barns? Stables? They'll burn them! And will they work? Will they stay forever? Surely they'll steal and vandalise everything, then murder us in our beds! That's what they're doing everywhere. Must we commit suicide because they're too lazy to provide for themselves? I will not agree to a soup kitchen in our courtyard, Robert, and, if you do, I'm leaving. Immediately.

Field Marshal Knoggs piping. Must I follow?

4 April 1848

Nothing equals what we loved as children. We didn't know then how all things begin and end, like a tale, a shower of rain, a star, a life. Early April sun on the garden walls. Astonishing. Worth being alive to see. To walk and look. Why do we weep at beauty? The skull

The Landlord

behind? Lost happiness? The coming dark? Nothing to fear from nothingness, is there? This island should be Europe's garden, not its graveyard. More and more reminds me of India. Swarming humanity, famine and filth, palaces and pigsties, a wretched Eden more garrisoned, troubled and troublesome than all India. Here I was born though, grew up and, despite famine, horror and hatred, it's where I'd choose to die and be buried. Unlikely now.

6 April 1848

Called at the poorhouse again. Murphy still hiding away. Sounds less unhinged. Put my head into the yard privies on the way out. Even a thousand paupers shat there today they shouldn't smell so foul. Crap pits could have been built over barrows for dragging straight to the fields. Romans doing that before Christ, the Chinese before that. Wilkinson's fault. Wretched, puffed up architect.
—Clearing them out'll give them something to do, he said.
Shoddy jobwork. No imagination. I implied as much last time he was here.
—Would you like a paupers' billiard hall, my Lord? A ballroom? A few tennis courts? A croquet lawn perhaps?
Touchy man. Went on to say the first poorhouses in England were designed as houses of terror, and that John Russell, the PM himself, had admired 'the humane and frugal grace' of his plans.
—It would be difficult, I said, to imagine anything more frugal. I could have added 'Or more inhuman'.
He noted that. Swilling down my claret, apropos of nothing he said,
—What ruins most landscapes from here to Moscow are these brute erections with their balls up on gatepillars shouting: 'Behold me, little people! See my big windows,

my big doors, my ice-house, my artificial lake!' Makes for bad architecture and worse politics!
After quite a silence I asked,
—Would you include Versailles?
—In particular Versailles.
—Its gardens?
—Worse again.
What gardens, I asked, did he most admire?
—Any cottier's vegetable patch, anywhere.
Tin-made spouting. Middle-class jealousy. What the French revolution was mostly about. Won't eat with me again. His plans used all over Ireland. The outskirts of every other town. Grim bastilles of despair. Imagines himself a radical reformer. An obtuse idiot. Could have, but didn't, return rudeness for rudeness.

10 April 1848

Murphy opened his door today. A hollow-eyed ghost. Still not eating much. Drinking a lot, I'd guess. Slow speech and the stricken look.
—More fitting, I said, to drink yourself to death at my age than yours!
No response. Hinted the poorhouse was disorderly without him. Hanratty a sort of mock-priest creeping about, a telltale with no authority. An irritant to board and paupers.
—That fellow couldn't run a hen run, I said.
No response. Went on to tell him we were alike with a sister apiece. Mine, Judy, the older by four years. As youngsters she'd pinch and punch for no reason, then smother me with kisses and beg me not to tell. This I thought the female way, till one day she taunted,
—You'll be a Lord, my Lord, when you grow up!

The Landlord

You'll get a whole barony because of your little bits!

Then grabbed my testicles and squeezed till I screamed.

Yet again I didn't tell. 'Just a lark,' she said. Sensing her dislike, I'd disliked her in return. From then on began to hate her and continued hating till I could hit back. End of ear-twisting and bullying. You don't forget such things, though I did promote her husband, young Gillespie. Arrogant ass. Disobeyed Wellington and got himself court-martialled.

Murphy listening. No effect. I went further. Pointed through his window towards the canal.

—If she was drowning in that lock I'd be tempted to walk away!

Still no response. Irrational grief. Didn't want to put it blunt as that so asked him,

—What are you in mourning for? A three-year-old child or a strange woman who cursed you?

Finally he looked at me with something akin to hatred. The longer I live the less I understand the human heart. My own included.

12 April 1848

The *Times* today. Two figures, one fact.

1780: Population of Ireland. Two and a half millions.

1845: Population of Ireland. Nine millions plus!

Some seven million tenants at will. And who squeezes the rent from these poor creatures? Agents! Middle-class middle-men, gombeen men, all prospering, all mostly Irish! And the emergent Church of Rome now building like beavers all over the island. Free labour and farthings of the poor. Every Chapel on a higher site than the Protestant Church. Nearer My God to Thee? Elevated thinking!

The Galligan priest's a surly rascal. Knows something

or pretends to. Long ago I'd have flogged the half smile off his face or marched him into an ambush. Or thought about it!

14 APRIL 1848

Stood at the bedroom window a long time this morning. Again a low mist on the lake, thorn ditches a glory of white. Fields of thriving cattle and sheep as far as I could see. Land of green and plenty. Brairds of winter oats and wheat, squads of men with spades, slipes and horses. Drain digging and barrowing of stones. Pastoral peace. Or seeming? Work till dark this time of year. For whom, now? All ending soon.

Draft for July edition of the *Farmer's Gazette* came yesterday. Hid letter till now. Heartbreak to read and look out on what must go. My approval for the following requested. Eyes filling as I read:

DAY OF SALE FIXED
Fermanagh Barony on the market.
W. W. Simpson has the honour to announce by order of the noble proprietor, at the Royal Hotel Belfast on Wed 7th of July at 11 a.m. sharp, the sale of Eden Hall Estate comprising circa 20,000 Irish acres including the townlands of Drumbofin, Burdautien, Cooldarra.

And on it went naming, mapping, describing. Know every bush and tree, ditch and sheugh, lake and river bend. The shape of every field, forest and meadow. Can't believe they're printed out. For sale. End of everything. How do I walk a hundred townlands, my heart breaking? Who'll buy? Whose eyes see what I see when I

The Landlord

waken to the light of this morning's wonder? A Belfast cattle shipper? A Dublin corn merchant? A builder from Cork? My heart stops at the thought. Neighbours will see it with a chill and think, Well, it's not us yet!

And when they gather next they'll say,

—See old Clonroy's in the *Gazette*?

—Surprising! Wife has no end of money, they say!

Won't care much. Leslie maybe. Likes me well enough. Says we think alike. We don't. O'Connell and native politics! A parliament of cattle dealers and bank clerks, ruled by a rookery of priests plotting our downfall! Squabbling over who'll rule a mess of beggars! No. No. No. I'd prefer Birmingham to that! Talked to me once about our rights here being suspect.

—Nothing here when we arrived, I said, but bush, bog and plain.

—And the native Irish! he said.

—We drained bogs and marshes, made roads. What's suspect about building mills and manor houses, towns and villages? We civilised it. I refuse to be guilty about that.

He smiled. Swift lodged there. And O'Connell.

Given half a chance he'd patronise the Pope.

16 April 1848

Murphy out and about again. Almost genial in his morose way. Very out of character showed me lines from *The Nation* written by some poet who died young.

> 'I have seen death strike so fast
> That churchyards could not hold
> The bright-eyed and the bold.
> I must be very, very old,
> A very old, man.'

He watched me reading and said,
—That's how I feel.

Clearly not himself yet. Can't tell anyone how I feel about selling. Not merely old, but desolate betimes. Tells me the third burial pit's near full. Two and a half thousand dying every week now from Malin to Dingle. Workhouse figures only. God alone knows how many more unrecorded, unburied out through the islands, mountains and bogs. Last year he was all for burning our dead in the grounds, out of sight of the paupers. Corpses fouling the water. Could be right. Galligan, for the Roman Church, said wrong. A desecration. Some claptrap about resurrection of the body. Too inane to argue over.

Parsee 'towers of silence' near Bombay. There they put their dead high up on grids. Chimney stacks of the dead. Vultures then flopping out of the mangos, circling around and up, to feast. I watched, appalled. Their bones picked clean in the sun. We choose slow rot in the earth, rats and worms nesting in our bowels. No great choices. All the one.

18 April 1848

What is wrong? Who's to blame? What to do? All newspapers, gazettes and journals, wheeling out these questions every other day. *Times* quoting the silly Wilde woman's whining doggerel:
 'A ghastly spectral army, before the great God we'll stand
 And arraign ye as our murderers, the spoilers of our land.'
Crazy. I know the answer in a word, or two. Daren't print for fear of being shrieked down by the patriot press. *Improvidence. Congenital improvidence.*

The Landlord

Devil-me-care, happy-go-lucky children. Next week's a hundred years off. When they get money every farthing's gulped in shebeens and pissed out in sheughs. Raving lunatics then, reciting and bellowing out dismal ballads about lost battles, dispossession, and glorious Celtic past! Drunken and shifty living in shit with pigs and fowl! Christ alone knows the swarming incest rife in those wretched hovels! How otherwise? Blame us for that too? Of course.

What about Rome? Manufacturing and baptising hundreds of thousands of impoverished wretches. The whole family caboodle in the image and likeness of God! Catholic clergy plays a wily part in general disaffection. Preach against rebellion. Skilled at saying one thing means the other. Galligan, a sample. Curate at Strokestown before here. His PP, McDermott, likened young Mahon to Oliver Cromwell, knowing full well most Irishmen would kill each other for honour of killing Cromwell. Exit Denis Mahon with a bullet in his head, as decent a reforming landowner as ever drew breath. Murdered with Rome's blessing.

Then all the back somersaulting in aftermath. Condemnation and denial. The handwashing of guilt in crocodile tears. Unholy terrors. Know their capers inside out. Seamus Shillelagh, the skull basher, shakes his ruggy head.

—A bad doin', your honour, to be sure.

If they fear 'the smile of an Englishman', let all of English blood beware the Hibernian headshake.

20 April 1848

Edmund Spenser, poet to the Virgin Queen. A great Irish hater. Small wonder. His children burned one night by

Irish rebels. Kilcolman Castle. Surviving grandson flirted with Popery. Lands escheated by Cromwell. Banished to Connaught despite plea by Lord Deputy. Dot's nightmare. Hates it when I used Irish with Mathew.

—It sounds rude, it is rude!

In Russia, I said, landowners and serfs speak the same language. A bond. Like one great family. Revolution most unlikely there. Dangerous to be alienated by language as we are here.

She stared blinking and asked,

—What language did the Sans Culottes speak? Chinese?

—Went on to talk about a Seigneur Memmay of Quincey. Knowing the great chateaus were burning all over France he invited the whole countryside to a banquet. Laid on barrels of wine and gunpowder. Blew them and his chateau to kingdom come and disappeared. An ugly parable, I said. Did *she* admire Seigneur Memmay?

—He stole a march on the enemy. Thought as a soldier, you'd admire that!

22 April 1848

Stringer, our Church of Ireland man, eavesdropped on Galligan's preaching. Wrote out what he overheard.

Life has conquered, the wind has blown away
Alexander, Caesar and all their power and sway,
Tara and Troy have made no longer stay.
Maybe the English too will have their day.

Then a long, unchristian diatribe which ended,

Brothers and sisters in Christ, Spain got shut of the Moors after fourteen hundred years. The English are

The Landlord

only here six and their time's near done. Soon you'll look down from above on an Ireland that once again belongs to us, free of English, free of landlords, free of agents, free of bailiffs, free of house tumblers. Our day will come.

Will it? If a pauper myself sitting with no hope, on a bench in an Ulster poorhouse, mid-nineteenth century, waiting for death, that would, I suppose, lift my spirits a little. Our day will come! Will it?

—All men are born equal and everywhere in chains!

Yah! The same Rousseau ran off and left his wife and five children 'in chains'. Penniless. A bloody rascal — like Bonaparte, like most 'heroes'.

23 April 1848

Whatever the cause, famine has prowled this island since God knows when, and will, till kingdom come. April to August. 'The hungry months.' Half a million starving more or less every year. Now with blight it's multitudinous, a nation of diseased scarecrows, swarming on centuries of beggary. Out of the townlands into the towns, cities and villages, down from the mountains to crowd out ports and seashores. Beggars huddled and huddles of beggars, all ages and stages. What happens when you see incurable beggary year in, year out? Indifference? Can't admit to that!

24 April 1848

Went to attic bin to check on last year's diary. There *he* was, exactly one year back, 24 April 1847. The giant, genius of 'Freedom'! Great Saviour of the world!

—With the stroke of a pen, he said, I will end all famines. As gifted as a hundred gifted men but a monumental hypocrite. Curious to re-read now what I dreamt a year ago.

Pissing into his cocked hat on horseback. Laughing at gravediggers deep in Russia. Dead Frenchmen piled in heaps. Death no laughing matter I told him. Asked him had he no shame. He shrugged and said,

—I'm trying to make a new world. You're starving the old one to death.

As he galloped off I shouted after him,

—Emperor, my arse! You're a relic, man, a relic!

Damn nearly wet the bed. Too much port? Ageing bladder more like. Seventy-two next week. Old. No way out of that but one. Why 'relic'?

Read on as far as the midsummer entries, now called BLACK '47. Worse than plague. Indescribable. Every other day the odour of blight mentioned. *Phytophthora infestans.* Death smell. Death knell, more like. All over. Terrible reports. Every province. Towns, townlands, villages, cities, and seashores. All heading for the ports and America. God help them. Will He? Will America? Can anyone? Poorhouses a wretched answer.

Last year's brief entry for

21 JUNE 1847

Poor Law rates long overdue. Dorothy paid. Festus Daly on the lawn. Croquet.

The start of an unlucky history, in those thirteen words. Bank had said no to second mortgage. Dot helped out. Lump sums fatten her account from Birmingham and

The Landlord

elsewhere. As chairman and biggest landowner all starving poor lodged in new poorhouse to my account. Six hundred and eighty-seven paupers last year at four pounds per annum, per pauper. Can't be done. Has me near pauperised. Irish Squireen's refusing to pay. As RM I have no choice.

—Festus Daly on the lawn. Croquet!

Grotesque memory! *Humanitas infestans*. Who was Saint Festus? Yet another Irish 'saint' topping up the provender of Hibernian sanctity. Face like an axe, voice like a rasp. 'Festy Waterloo' they call him hereabouts. Sounds quaint. Not so quaint with his wooden leg and Basque beret. Tenant in a rough, mountainy area. Bragan country. A Bonaparte veteran. Composite of everything that's worst or 'best' in the Irish character. Depending on viewpoint. On losing side at Waterloo. Walked drunk onto the croquet lawn that evening. Challenged me!

—Gun or sword, Skinner, I'll bate you with aither.

'Escorted' off he got, shouting out,

—I'm better bred than you, Skinner, a better soldier and a proper Irishman, and you mind that!

I said I'd bear it in mind. Farcical request before thirty guests. In every barony of Ireland they're descended from Kings or High Kings. You can see that at a glance! All thought it, 'Very Irish, immensely amusing'.

Shirley of Castle Fea begged me to mimic the accent and manner. I refused. Could have, with the Irish I've had since childhood.

—Learn every inflection, son, my father said. More practical than going about armed to the teeth with bodyguards you can't trust.

Shrewd advice. Hard to kill a man who can curse, sing, dance and tell jokes in the language. But came back an ex-general, peer and landlord. Embellishments not popular here. Not hated though, the way Leitrim is, or Lansdowne, but I do keep German shepherds. Dot keeps wolfhounds. Great, silly brutes wolfing down bones and offal. Obscene, these famine days, with no wolves left to hunt. My German shepherds a must for night watches, and my steel shutters and gun room with its cast iron door. A necessity. Siege clobber of caste.

I'm a soldier. I know men, especially Irishmen. I didn't think Daly amusing.

—Dangit, and the landlord's the quare bad lad, so he is. He's the boy I'd hang, so I would!

And he would. Cut my throat or put a bullet in my brain without a shrug. Something not sane in those bulging eyes, something not sane about the whole race. Belligerent, resentful, capricious, treacherous. Uncivil citizens. Worse servants, with the odd exception. The Murphys with us here two hundred years. His father my batman in Calcutta, more friend than servant. Died aboard ship on the way home. Saddest of sad events. Saved my life once, his own at risk. That's more that loyalty.

Read on looking for second tangle with Festus. Found it painful reading.

Gale Day, September 1847

Agent's office. Daly came in sober, wearing his Basque beret. As he put his rent on the nail Sammy Agnew said,

—Bare your head, Daly, in Lord Clonroy's presence!

—He's gettin' his rent. Why should he view my head?

Agnew then snatched at Daly's beret, who caught his arm and twisted it up till his face gouged onto the rent table. He then put his backside over Agnew's mouth and said,

—You can view up there any time you like, Sammy!

Jerked his peg leg up at me, he added,

The Landlord

—You too, Mister Skinner!
I could have ended it there by saying,
—Let him wear his beret, Sammy. I don't want to 'view' his head or his arse!
I pulled the bellcord for Dowler and Bailey. From the landing window saw Daly being thrown out, held, punched and kicked on the ground. His wooden leg came off. He grabbed it and pointed up at Agnew mouthing savagely. Seldom seen such hatred in a human face. Should have stopped it. Or tried to. I was angry. A mistake.

30 SEPTEMBER 1847

History lesson for poor student. Act of Union. The Britannic Islands. 1800. John Bull bulling his rebellious daughter. Outraged by her defiance and hatred. Violates her even more. Like it or not, it seems like that. No mean violater myself!

31 DECEMBER 1847

Sammy Agnew found this morning hanging from an apple tree. Agent's garden. What a year's end! Hard to imagine anything more savage. Whole house, village and barony deeply shocked. Signed with Daly's brutal signature. Pock marks from his peg leg under the apple tree. A bright, glorious winter's day. Made it somehow more grotesque. Nightmare again. Bonaparte pointing and smiling.

7 March 1848

Day of sale fixed.
Fermanagh Barony on the market.
W. W. Simpson has the honour etc.
Wed 7th of July at noon.
The noble proprietor.

A Belfast salesroom. Four months from now. Days falling off one by one. The hand bids one by one. Then the hammer like a guillotine. The end.

Nathaniel Skinner came here land-hungry 1612. From English/Scottish borderlands. Old Irish scattered. His blood abiding in me beside this lake. Same walled garden, same apple trees, oldest in Ulster. Our own church and graveyard. No wish to be buried elsewhere.

Attachment to place means little to Dot. Seems unaware of what it means to me. Indifferent almost. At the start though, spent lavishly. Re-roofed house and stables, built a water tower, new entrances. Miles of enclosing wall. Gave employment. Also gained her deeds to house, grounds and gardens. Entitlement to change the name. First dwelling here was in townland of Drumbofin. Ancient placename.

—What does it mean, Robert, Drumbofin?

—The ridge of the white cow, I said, and the O sounds like the O in low.

—What it means is more ridiculous than how it sounds!

I protested. A necklace of townlands connected to estate. I named some, explained their meaning. Tamlaght, Rathclough, Inishglora, Mullinamuck, Gola, Drumlanna, Largy, Tubberlucas.

She didn't like any of them and opted for Eden Hall. Very Birmingham to my ears, I said. She took exception to that.

The Landlord

—Eden, she said, is paradise, and paradise is from the Arabic, meaning a walled garden. I'd prefer that to places called after cows, pigs, or goats, or wells!

—What objection, I asked, did she have to Oxford or Tunbridge Wells?

—They don't sound spineless.

No arguing with fixed prejudice. Well educated but understands very little. Or very differently. None of it matters now. If it ever did.

8 March 1848

Daly had foolproof alibi. Got off. Predictably. By law, now, three Catholics on every jury a legal obligation. Unless all three witnessed him string up Sammy Agnew they'd never find against. That makes nine agents and six landlords assassinated this past twelve months. Nobody got for them. With huge police force and standing army big as India's the Dalys are still at large all over Ireland. Rebellion and famine hand in hand. Heard Leitrim mutter his drunken solution at Dartry:

—Bloody Irish, bloody awful. Let them starve!

17 March 1848

Looked up 'Skinner' in Johnson. 'A flayer of beasts, scum of pools, pelt or hide of animals.' Also he gives thickskin, thinskin and scarfskin. Quotes Shakespeare:

>'Authority, though it err like others,
>Has yet a kind of medicine in itself,
>That skins the vice o' th' top.'

The big monkey steals the big banana. Bonaparte marched into Switzerland. Gobbled their gold. The world secretly applauded. Wretched Swiss Bankers. Theft canonised by Crown and Church and State the world over. Father toyed with notion of deed polling Skinner to Scarfe. Act of Union bribe netted a peerage. Tittle, tittle, tattle, title and, hey presto, look ye, poor Skinner's glorified to Clonroy!

And thanks be to God for that, Lady Clonroy said. Growing up Dot Knoggs was bad enough. To be Mrs Bob Skinner would have been insupportable. Formerly Dorothy Knoggs, only child of Sir George Knoggs, Gin Distiller, Birmingham. Very much her father's daughter. He trundled down streets with a barrow. Ended up with a distillery. Flung so much loot at the Tories they dubbed him Sir George. Early on, when we came back from India, she said,

—If you can't make this property pay, Robert, we should sell and go to Birmingham.

I can't make it pay, but *we* should sell it and go somewhere like Eden Place, Daddy George's mock baronial edifice. Talks now of ending her days in like setting. More dignity in a Bath lodging house. Let me not think on it!

20 March 1848

Famine if anything worse than this time last year.

The improvidence of my neighbour, Johnson says, must not make me inhuman.

Of course not. Who are mine? Leslie and Shirley? Wyndham and Farnham? Erne, Leitrim and Enniskillen? With quarter of a million acres between us! And out there, beyond our walls, out of sight, but never out of mind, that swarming otherness, that Irishness, their hatred fuelled by disease, famine, and death. Out there is

The Landlord

hell. In here, where I live, is heaven! Is it? Life with Field Marshal Knoggs! Did mutter once, as a general the lives of thousands in my care. Tinkered on two continents with arms and discipline, training and logistics, strategy, purveying, budgeting, medical field-care, and some other details. She laughed.

—Your underlings did *that* for you, Robert!

—Odd they should make me a general?

—Because you look and sound like somebody.

Thanked her for commending my phonics and physiognomy. Irony lost on her. Like anyone with purse strings. Tends to the capricious. Brutal worldly truth. A man of meagre banking account is a man of little or no account. So dance to her jig, me Lord, and be happy you're not a bare-arsed pauper starving in a poorhouse. Murphy's mad solution. Become a pauper myself! In a way I am. Pauperised.

21 March 1848

The word 'underling' squatting in my brain since yesterday. Sees me as a hollow vessel, does she? Does it matter at my age? As others see us? Valid both ways. The Ball in Calcutta where wives of high ranking officers refused place in a booked carriage to young Captain's wife who fell ill. Rank cruelty.

Dot sided with senior ladies. Bitches conscious of station and lacking all dignity. Was appalled and said so. Argument then. As a ginmonger's daughter she would naturally, I said, be grander in manner and mind than a Duchess.

Greatly resented. Suddenly got silly and went, 'Law Di Daw, Law Di Daw!' like a Birmingham street urchin.

—And where did the noble Skinners hail from? she

asked. Skinning dead animals in a shambles?

Still rankles twenty years on. And still comes up.

23 March 1848

Bonaparte back again to mock my sleep? Greed and grandeur? Far from grand when he's off his horse. Fat, dumpy fellow with small feet walking the shore of a tiny island. Billy goats bleating at him. The Upper Lough? Wearing dancing pumps, a greatcoat and silly hat. Talking to himself. Staring out at the water through a telescope. His 'Empire' cut to nothing. When he turned to look at me it was *my* baggy bloodhound eyes I was looking into. Me, is he? All men?

—I know men, he said, and Jesus Christ was no man!

Who then was He? Is He? The Man God not of this world, friend to whores and halfwits, corpse raiser, water walker, promiser of a kingdom no one's ever seen. Thy kingdom come?

Mine's earmarked for the *Farmer's Gazette*. July. That much is certain.

27 March 1848

Leitrim evicted a cottier refused to salute his horses clopping down through his village. All must grovel when he passes in person. Being a lord and landowner not enough. Bonaparte made the Pope grovel, forced a penstroke through six hundred years of inquisition. A genius for good as well as self glory. Leitrim an untalented bully. Insane, degenerate.

The Landlord

28 March 1848

A large rat near the poorhouse bakery. Pushed his way through a cracked flag. Fat, sick and wet. I stood very still, staring. He was so close, so unafraid, I could see him blinking, nose and whiskers twitching in my direction.

—Don't blink at me, brother, I said quietly. I'm no pauper, not on your menu yet!

When he didn't move I shouted,

—Run, rat, run! Back to the burial pit! You can feast there for a hundred years! And keep away from the living, Sir, the half living, and half dying!

Nobody about. Odd, a bit, shouting out like that in a poorhouse yard? Thought I'd be unaffected, but watching him squeeze down through that crack, tail slithering after, gave me a sudden shiver. And dry mouth. Yet another premonition of mortality? What else? Death now a constant companion. Partly what brought me back. No longer hiding up a tree or round a bend. Alongside peering from a rathole. Best be on friendly terms when it turns to blink.

—You are welcome, Sir? Madam? Rat? I've been expecting you. May I ask where we're going?

30 March 1848

Clarendon with us again en route to Belfast. Unassuming and kind. Affects everyone. Asked to see kitchen staff to thank in person. Dot says more likely wanted to see if it was clean as Viceregal Lodge! First time I've been below stairs in God knows when. He's more interested in landscape and woodland than wheels and spokes of politics.

I pointed out conifers, hardwoods and block plantings

to echo battle lines at Waterloo. Hugely interested. Or pretended. Told me John Russell treated him last year like a sub-post office clerk at Number 10. Behaved as though rebellion and famine here had little to do with London. Then snapped suddenly,

—I'm sorry if your Irish landlords and agents are being shot like hares, Clarendon, but I can't pretend to be shocked. Our people here aren't evicting whole villages into the jaws of winter. Migrating by the hundred thousand! Our big-hearted friends in America are now closing their ports. They can! We can't! From now on we'll let your Irish landlords support the paupers they evict, not the British treasury.

—Then you'll bankrupt them, Prime Minister, almost all.

—Probably, Russell said. Deservedly. Was there ever a more hated class?

Deservedly! I know we're mostly despised over there and certainly hated here but I'm no villain. I've no secret wish to evict, hang, starve or transport the poorest of the poor which some are accusing us of. Nor did I know the Tories had disowned us as a class.

1 April 1848

Since Clarendon's visit the message from Russell hasn't left my head.

—We'll make your Irish landlords pay!

A litany of five words in my head, awake or asleep.

—I am pauperised by paupers, I am pauperised by paupers, I am pauperised by paupers.

The Landlord

5 April 1848

Inclined to count things. Words, steps, chimneys, hayrucks, turfclamps, paupers. Counted seven magpies this morning on the front lawn. What tale hasn't been told? Doubtful if anything in this world, this island, this family, could surprise me now.

7 April 1848

Stringer preached a long sermon. Church cold. The 'Son of Man' paraded for endless edification. God knows how many times he uttered it. Silly wording. Son of Man. Son of a child-bearing male? Keep females out. Not so easy when it comes to procreation. Does he believe the pious nonsense he preaches? Does anyone? Certainly doesn't practise. Not a word to his daughter Norma since she married Fitzpatrick, the Papish corn merchant.

8 April 1848

One full year into the famine and things seem worse. How to cure poverty? By feeding? Insane! By ignoring? Heartless. Teach them to provide for themselves. If they refuse they're digging their graves. If we feed them we're digging ours. Like other landowners, if they forgo their plots I pay passage to America, to anywhere. For years I told my cottiers God created a hundred vegetables for us to live on. Surely you can grow enough to feed yourselves and your families. How do they answer? They fall on their knees and whine,
 —We have no brains, your honour, to grow vegetables like gentlefolk. Only the praties, your honour.

Prátaí i maidí
Prátaí san ló
Agus ma éiríghim san oíche
Prátaí a geobhainn.

Christ in heaven what's to be done with such people?

Last year I bought seeds. Turnip, mangold, carrot, cabbage, and kale, cauliflower, parsnip and leeks. I translated the instructions. How to sow, thin, weed, mulch, water, routine horticultural stuff. A child of five could do it, then saw what they tried or didn't! A mess of weeds in lazy beds!

—Bad seeds, your honour, a poor strike, your honour! The slugs ate them, your honour! I lost them, your honour! The crows ate them, your honour.

The pigeons, rabbits, squirrels, daws, magpies, rats and mice, all regiments of the vermin world converging on one pratie plot! And who's to blame? The landlords of Ireland! Convenient to have a bogeyman to flog for everything that goes wrong in life!

9 April 1848

Called today on the curate, Galligan. Old PP in the corner. Glared at me in silence. McKenna. Looks quite mad. Smell of bacon and cabbage. Slated foursquare house like strong farmer's. God's earthy agents. Pigs grunting out the back. Glossy bullocks on front pasture. Oil portraits of Bishop of Rome and Clogher between gilt-framed Madonna, eyes rolling upwards, hands over virginal quiver, feet crushing serpent's head. Obscene effect.

Can't see what's in front of them. More ways than one. Explained the merits of vegetable varieties, how you must be diligent and work. Can't put tiny seeds in the

The Landlord

ground and forget like 'praties'. Would they talk about this at Sunday Mass? With the hungry months now upon us a matter of grave urgency for cottiers to grow alternatives. Blight bad as last year.

They listened, with reserve. 'Perfidious Albion'? Am I? Fatheads! How could vegetable growing be a landlord's trap? Thundering every other Sunday, both of them, about God's 'punishment' for being natural. Coupling in ditches mostly. Marry at sixteen. Ten years later, enormous families living in starving squalor! They're the bogeymen with their pigs and bullocks, their black suits and dog collars.

11 April 1848

High Court in Dublin today. Daly got his hands on Daniel O'Connell. God knows how. Unlucky to have Judge Liam O'Hanrahan presiding. Cold eye, colder smile. Ruled there was no law obliging a man to bare his head while paying rent. O'Connell played to gallery. Festus described as 'A noble warrior maimed in cause of liberty'! I was derided as 'Lord Hatsoff, a neighbour Lord of the Lord who likes his horses to be saluted'! Uproarious laughter. Reprimanded for 'Domineering behaviour'. Fined a shilling and costs. O'Connell's fee, fifty guineas! The patriot press no doubt will be vindictive and jubilant.

13 April 1848

Chaired third last meeting of Poorhouse Guardians. When advertisement appears it must close. Said nothing. Murphy quiet. Deferential to Galligan. Surprising. His view of Romishness more jaundiced than mine. After the meeting Galligan caught my sleeve, closed boardroom door. Did I know the Bradys of Drumlanna? Impossible not to. The orphan girl walks like a ballet dancer, her mother a sister of Festus Daly's. Same mad eyes. Confined to idiot ward like a trapped hare. Murdered her granddaughter, they say.

—They're tenants of mine, I said. Drumlanna's the next townland.

—Ex-tenants, he said. Evicted. Their house was tumbled and burned.

—Because of typhus. Mister Murphy went out of his way to place them here.

—Murphy, he said, was using the girl, and may again.

—In what way? I asked.

—The only way a man in his position can.

—Did she complain?

—No.

—Confess, perhaps?

He reacted very sharply to this. Overstepped the mark? Insulting implication? Sacred seal. All sins go straight from his ear to God's. Shrewd information dodge. Of course I knew the Bradys. Father's bloodshot eyes and trembling hands. Shouldn't have asked him to tailor breeks for Clarendon. Probably gave them away to the first bare-arsed beggar he met.

15 April 1848

Mathew arrived this evening with young Dixon and the two Gilmartin girls. Both redheads. Gigglers both. The younger full-breasted as a springing heifer. Leaning forward at table to show them off. A freckled beauty. There was talk about some child running alongside the carriage on last visit. I wasn't here. Mathew's tone cool

The Landlord

and accusing. Dot didn't know. Or pretended. Greek meets Greek. His cold temper a match for her blazing one. He hasn't changed. Dismissive about almost everything.

Seems I sleepwalked into the blue bedroom where the younger girl was sleeping. Tried to get in beside her. A lot of crying out and hysteria. The whole house up, staff running with cudgels and candles. No sign of Mathew or young Dixon. Wherever they were. I made matters worse by saying,

—Do excuse me. Thought this was an army-licensed brothel.

Dot very cross. No memory of anything. Refused to believe it till I was shown my slippers in the blue room. More and more inclined to stray by night. By day as well. Is the head going? Searching for something? My grave? Lost youth? Virgin breasts? Pray God I die before Birmingham. What a lucky exit that would be. At seventy-three.

17 April 1848

Very glad to be shut of young Dixon's staring hero-worship. Hanging on Mathew's every word. Do those girls or Dot have the faintest notion? He got me alone in the kitchen garden. Told me he'd been accepted for a Jesuit seminary in Spain. Somewhere near Zaragosa. Convert to Church of Rome. Kept my face like a boot. Asked me not to tell his mother. Yet. No great surprise. Always inclined to playacting and dressing up. Prep school a hotbed for that inclination. Most graduate to females. Clearly he didn't. Conversion to Rome I did not expect. Jesuits will love him till they catch him out. Unless they're at the same caper themselves and turn the blind eye like Nelson. Like I had to, in the army.

19 April 1848

Up very late drinking port with Mathew. Not by choice. Spiky conversation.

—No famine here, he said. Plenty of food. Ports should be closed and people fed.

—How? I asked. Who'd pay?

By way of answer he shrugged and said,

—It's what Bonaparte would have done.

During a silence I got the draft advertisement for the *Farmer's Gazette*. Foolish. He read it without expression of interest or regret and said,

—Just as well. We're not wanted here.

—Perhaps we're needed?

—For what?

—To run the country.

—You think?

—I do.

—The way we're running it now?

Stared at me the way the slightly drunk do. Each word as it came slowly out seemed framed.

—They might just manage without us.

His patrimony and half a millennium of rule dumped with half a dozen words. Indifference more hurtful than contempt. I can hide what I feel. May even have smiled. Have always known he wanted no link with pastoral life. Later in the night he said,

—Military people are mostly bullies dressed up to kill.

—Like Bonaparte?

—Yes, like Bonaparte.

—And he'd close the ports, would he?

—Yes, he would.

Preachy and contradictory. The Roman Church will suit him well. I stood. Went to bed without another word.

27 April 1848

How to convey Mathew's intentions to Dot. She keeps him supplied with money. Has never said this, but I know it. She'll be baffled, angry.

—But Rome is evil, she'll say.

Far from Christ, I'll agree, and remind her about 'England's hallowed walls founded on King Henry's balls'. Our Church here the poor eunuch over the water. Would God bother His celestial arse with either? Or with Rome, Constantinople, Avignon, or a hundred other variations? Christianity as much to do with Christ as a pack of dogs snarling over their own vomit. Won't say that, though. A believing person, Dot. Or pretends. So am I!

28 April 1848

Mathew in my head night and day. His defection makes selling easier. No heir now but Judy's stupid boy. Prefer to sell on. Three months left.

29 April 1848

Yet another tangle with Festus. Came in the form of a blackmail letter delivered by a stableboy. Said he'd found it in a manger. It was addressed to *'The Skinners, father and son'*.

I opened it. We read together. I glanced once at Mathew's face as I read. It was chalky white.

'First and last warning to Mathew Skinner bugger be gone a week from this day we have heerd tell of your bad carry on a stableboy complained you did a bugger on

him and was afeard to say no to a gentleman the likes of you it was a bad thing you done to that poor boy and not a dam thing can put it right when it come to our ears we lit on a cure from the old days and a sure one it is a red hot poker goes in to the buggers arse hole he lets out one shout and its his last its a proper cure.'

I said nothing. He said nothing. I read his silence the only way I could. Thieving, gambling, whoring or passional murder I could have stomached. Not shaming the house by fouling innocence. Watch out for men who preach at you, including your own family! Especially your own family!

Dear God, what a reversal of shame. The radical hater of military bullies turns out to be a hypocrite. How could it be otherwise with Rousseau and Bonaparte as exemplars? Believe no one absolutely, ever. Trust no one absolutely, ever. Query everything. Bear in mind what's true today is false tomorrow and vice versa till the next Ice Age or kingdom dumb. Grow your carrots, mind your corner, and expect nothing much from this life or the next.

30 April 1848

Mathew left this morning. We embraced in the hall. It was cold. The embrace. Will I see him again, in this world? Doubtful. Do I want to? Doubtful. Must be heartbreak in that but can't feel it. Yet. Dot went out to wave him off. Wondered why I didn't. I made some reply, not sure what.

—Is Mathew in trouble of some sort? she asked. In debt?

To which I muttered,

—I wish he was.

The Landlord

—Has it to do with the history of this wretched island?
—It *is* the history, I said, of this wretched island.

The house seemed like a prison, all that careful building, the accumulation of centuries, tumbling now like a house of cards. I went out for air. Stayed out. No appetite, no wish to return to the house. Walked till dusk alongside the enclosing walls screening off what I'd no stomach to look at, hovels like rotten teeth in a green mouth, a silent countryside without cattle, sheep or fowl. Turfsmoke a reminder of whole families starving at the hearth. Am I deserting these fields, this house where I was born, this island I once so deeply loved, the speech I dreamt in as a child? And the people? I can ask the question now. Was there love ever, anywhere, at any time between the dispossessed and those who dispossessed?

At evening yard bell, saw squads of workers and horses heading back for the stables. Wanted badly to get outside the walls, revisit forbidden fields, townlands and river stretches where I'd played out of bounds before the walls went up. Dangerous now. Knew I couldn't leave by the front or back entrance without being seen. Had a key to a small access gate, opened it, and let myself out. Must have been walking a long time looking at places where I'd been happy. Stopped to listen to a murmur down by Gola where the river forks. Had swum there often as a cub with local lads, Jimmy the Goat, Fisty McDonagh, Nosey O'Hara and Farty Boyle. All dead now but Farty. I then realised it wasn't water I was hearing but the murmur of people. Wasn't sure what to expect. A council of Ribbonmen armed with cudgels and cleavers? Festus Daly binding them with oaths and orders? A nightwandering landlord a banquet to such a crew!

In the mood I was in I didn't care. I would greet death like an old friend. Was it a wake perhaps? People too frightened now of cholera and typhus to attend wakes.

Everywhere the dead buried secretly or left to nature in remote bogs or mountain areas.

Keeping to the shadow of the ditch I came to a small garden level with a cottage chimney. Could see down through a screen of thorn hedge to the street. I knew at once I was witnessing an 'American wake', a common thing these days in every other townland of the island.

Under a moon tattered with clouds the people looked spectral. Famished ghosts more than humans. Saw a young man moving through them, shaking hands with neighbours, embracing relations, lifting and kissing children. Then saw him whisper something to a young girl who left the gathering and stood below me under the garden bank. Out of sight, but I could hear her emotion as the mother held on to the son calling him her '*bábóg*', kissing his hands and eyes and begging him not to go. The professional keeners then began a lament for 'The Dead Traveller', an archaic rigmarole praising his noble deeds, his prowess of body, his beauty of soul. Near the end of this, as though at the bidding of a hidden master of ceremonies, the crowd drew back to form a circle leaving two men alone in the middle. It now became clear that these two were father and son, clear too that they could find neither words nor actions to match what they felt at that moment, until the father spoke,

—Face me now, son, in a step, for likely as not, it's the last step we'll take in this world together.

As I watched them, hands at their sides in the rigid folk manner, heads up, boots thumping the dirt street, eyes locked on each other's face, I saw that many in the circle were unable to keep watching and had to turn away and, remembering then my own son and how we had parted and how I would soon be leaving here forever, I, myself, was obliged to turn away and, although no stranger to mortality and grief, it seemed to me that never until that

The Landlord

moment had I fully understood the suffering of these people my own family had lived amongst for so long, and never before had I witnessed anything so affecting, so full of heartbreak, as that awkward, final dance of farewell.

The Mother

Reach me down comfort, O Virgin most powerful. Cover me with sleep and sleep and sleep till my eyes open at the feet of Christ.

Hail Mary, full of grace. Hail Grace, full of O'Hara, Pat O'Hara's Jimmy Ned up on my wee innocent.

—Don't let them near your hidey place, I warned them girls, 'cause there's men walkin' the world ready to slip in and strut off braggin' into black pongers.

The angel of the Lord declared, so he did. And more. And she was conceived, so she was. And the word was made flesh. A mystery, that's for certain. Yes. And thon's her bell. The Angelus, is it? House of gold. Near dark or light? Which?

Dead bell more like. Never quits here, nor the squeal of that deadcart. Jesus, who for? Me, Mary Josephine Brady, née Daly? And where am I? Why let on, when I know full well? Chained in with barrels of piss and shit and a go of cracked Bridies is where I am, a shambles shed of howls is where I am, a screamin' hell is where I am, the idiot ward of a poorhouse is where I am, and serve me right, may God in His mercy forgive me, and Mary, His Blessèd Mother, and all the saints in heaven. It's punishment, so it is. And what was it we done on You, Lord, made You punish us that way, blight our praties, turn Your head away, then turn it back to watch us starve and sicken, go mad and die? Our poor sins, was it? What

The Mother

harm did they do You? What harm? May God forgive me, a sinner, to throw contrary questions at the face of Glory.

Thy will be done.
Thy will be done.
Thy will be done.

Was it Your will that bitter blow in March broke my heart beyond all mendin', took my Grace, warped my Roisin's heart, made my foolish husband lave, and left me nothin' of home and happiness but this poor cracked thing I am, in this foul purgatory? Is that the price You'd have me pay, Lord, for a few stumbles? Or have I more to pay? Has the Landlord of Heaven a harder heart than Skinner of Drumbofin? Is there nothin' from this day out only death and burials, burials, burials?

Ah my love, my love, my Roisin Dubh, you wronged me, daughter.

I renounce the world, the flesh and the Devil.
I renounce the world, the flesh and the Devil.
I renounce the world, the flesh and the Devil.

Full of Grace and Roisin I was one time, twin beauties, and the Devil knows how. I warned them day in day out, so I did. God knows I did. Any night they'd creep in late from wake or dance I'd shout at them,

—Is it a pair of hoors I have for daughters? Go out wash yerselves, ye dirty clarts, ye have me shamed before the whole country. Have ye naither a titter of wit nor track of dacency?

Wore out I was tellin' them how your sins wing back to find you out in the old meadows, poor frighted crakes, runnin' and hidin' from the hook of God, and there's no half-wise body in the world but knows that for the truth. They paid no heed. No heed. No heed. And did she cry, the cratur, when the blood come, God help her, and when her monthly didn't I lost the head and got her by the ear and chained her above like a pedlar's monkey, well hid from the eyes of Maggie Scarlett and her like.

I did. So I did.

So I did.

So I did. God forgive me.

—No Mama, no Mama, please Mama, please!

Grace, disgrace.

Grace, disgrace.

Grace, disgrace.

I tongued and tongued her in mad tempers for givin' in to a fly article the like of O'Hara. My Roisin was too wide to be caught that way but I'd a nose for her capers, away with the boys behind the boar's shack where the young ones pair off, aye, let them do it on her belly or her bum, too choosy to let them in, silly wee ditch hoors the two of them, no wit and half the country famished. Oh Christ forgive me. It's got in sin they were, them girls; aye, troth they were, but such beauties naked or dressed forninst the like of Maggie Scarlett's lumps. Small wonder she's jealous.

Like swans, my two. Take the sight from your eyes, so they would. Gone now both. Under the earth, and over the sea. Oh the head was half gone or full gone that time they brought me here and tied me down.

A mistake I made, to be sure, a mistake, and aren't we all wise after blunders, and don't we all blunder on, and swear never again, and on we go again all forgot, or do any of us know what we're at when nature's hot or the head's bothered? Do we? Who was it chained my girleen up like a stray goat? Me? Asha who else, woman? Don't cod yourself when you know rightly it was yourself. Me, myself, the bespoke tailor's wife. Bespoke? Brady, is it? A sham article couldn't sew a shroud on a ghost?

Now my Dada, John Daly, was a proper man with a proper grip on God and the Devil on account of Canon

The Mother

McKenna with his fancy Leinster Irish couldn't twig the Kerry boys' confessions, them squads of travellin' chancers diggin' turnips for Lord Skinner. Put him on a chair in a dark sacristy and made him face away from the Kerrymen and translate their sins. Bound him over to secrecy.

'Holy John' the neighbours called him from that day out. 'Holy John' of Drumlanna and the people travelled from the Bragans and farther out to ask his blessin' or get the cure for this or that and then he got the name of a man whose touch could make a barren woman hold and that made him cross.

—No, no, no, no, no, no, no, no, and the more he no-ed the more they'd fall to their knees and beg and in the end he'd put his two hands on their heads and pray to the Virgin Mother and they got their babbies, the most of them.

Now there's a mystery. Fierce holy, he was, and strict with it.

—If you girls don't quit that I'll redden your arses!

For a fit of the giggles only, at the Rosary. And more than a growl it was. He meant it. We quit our giggles quick, so we did. No man for empty threats. Forever traipsin' to clergy with backdoor tattle.

'Blessèd John Bollox of Drumlanna!' That's what Festus called him, the only one of the boys ever to face up to him and hit back. Two of a kind, only Festus grew to hate him, his own father. We all loved Mama, red-eyed in turfsmoke and clabber, stooped all her days over pots till she tumbled into her grave at fifty like most poor weemen in the world. Where are you now, Mama, with your bad cough? Can you hear me? And Granny Maguire? And Granny's Granny and her Granny and her Granny and all the Grannies of a hundred thousand winters away back to the blind start of the world? Up in heaven, are ye all? God help yeer ghosts, wherever ye are. Poor weemen, their vennel of tears dried up in the latter end. In their poor graves with their lost babbies. Me with them soon. At peace. My Roisin's gone, the wee bitch. How could she accuse the way she did? Greedy for the nipple she was, right off. The other wee thing had to be coaxed to suck. And they grew that way, hard and soft, open and closed, warm and cauld, one tagged for life, the other for death. Aye.

Body of Christ. Communion soon from Galligan, the priest of God.

—The settle bed'll buy a coffin to bury her proper, he said. The chape one with the lath and cardboard bottom I got from MacManus in Chapel Street. 'Twas Maggie Scarlett's grunt I heard at the graveside.

—She'll have her arse through that in a week.

Cross-eyed auld sow across from me here suckin' on her broken pipe. Never look in her eye or let on I hear her jibes.

—That Murphy fella has your other daughter bow-legged, Brady. Take care she doesn't end up potbellied like the others!

That class of spite's aisy shrugged off, but when your own blood stares from hooded eyes accusin', that's a heartscald.

—Can you hear me, Mama? I can talk kindly with you any time I want. Queenie Donnelly you were, before you married.

Queen of Angels.
Queen of Patriarchs.
Queen of Prophets.
Queen of Apostles.
Queen of Martyrs.
Queen of Confessors.
Queen of Virgins.

The Mother

Queen of all Saints.
Queen conceived without original sin.
—How were we conceived, Mama, with you below in the settle bed and Dada above in the cockloft?
—Hands on from Holy John, Festus said.
Or maybe seven more Immaculate Conceptions, and we childer were shocked and laughed but didn't Nora Tom blurt this round the pot of spuds? Dada cut an ashplant and lashed Festus till he wasn't fit to scream and locked him in the byre for a week on cold stirabout and water. He come out like a ghost. After that he held his tongue. Couldn't get away from Drumlanna quick enough. All the boys left one by one. Festus for Scotland, then France; Michael and Joe for Amerikay. The three girls married hereabouts, bar me, Mary Josephine.
—The big hallion of a lassie, spit of the father, everyone said.
It was Sadie put about what was overheerd in Caffrey's shebeen.
—Imagine slavin' out all day with Holy John and then the Rosary and litanies at night and, after that, gettin' up on big Mary Joe! Any man fit for thon'd need to be part saint, part hoe boy, and part billy goat!
Cruel and true. There was no pad tramped to our door by young fellas lookin' to join with me at Drumlanna. Any man wanted me and the ten acres knew he'd have to live in and work out with the half priest, Holy John. They kept well away. Every now and then there was a new babby for Cissie, Sadie or Nora Tom. He must've heard me one night cryin' quiet after a christenin' I didn't go to. I couldn't. It was Sadie's fourth and her not twenty-two.
—What ails ye, daughter? he called down from the cockloft. I was too choked up to answer.
—You want your own babby? Am I right?

I was so shamed he twigged this I quit the cryin' of a sudden.

—You're far too good for any man, he said. But I'll find you one.

—I don't want that, Dada, I said. Please. I don't want that. I'd as lief lie my lone.

—You'll do what I say, daughter, quit the cryin' now, say your prayers and go to sleep.

I always done what he said. I prayed.

'From growth to age, from age to death,

Be Thy two arms here, oh Christ about me.'

Got stiff as he aged. The hinches. I did the outside work. He kept the kitchen and often, when I come down from mouldin' spuds on the bracken hill or up from the gut field mindin' geese or in from turnin' hay beyont in the church field, he'd tell me who'd come and gone and what news there was in the world. Them were happy times, happy, happy times. Just the two of us and not a cross word nor a dumb patch between us, ever.

Oh Jesus, the heartbreak in this place now to mind such happiness, our own ass to bring home turf before the days grew chill, and the way we'd fall on our knees at night to thank the Maker of stars for this world and its wonders. Aye God, You were good to us then, when I was a girsha, so You were, praise be, in them days before the blight, before that time I scrubbed for the Mercys at Bellaney. Twelve I was and worse nor here it was, them long corridors hung with bishops and holy pictures so lonely I'd count fields in my head could be reckoned from our street at Drumlanna where you'd see sheep and goats and donkeys and hear childer in townlands as far off as Ballagh that I walked to once under the stars drunk with wonder at the sky and, anyway, I knew worse had befallen others than skivvyin' a year for nuns, up at five on my knees scrubbin' in the kitchen or emptyin' their

The Mother

chamberpots and them on their knees prayin' and prayin' great wheens of prayer for the souls of sinners and all the pagans in the world lost to God's mercy, and the time I cried out when it scalded me to pee and Reverend Mother come close with her witherdy face.

—Were you at yourself, girl?
—What, Mother?
—Don't pretend.
—I've no notion what —
—Immodestly? Tell the truth.
—I was not.
—If that's a lie and your bladder bursts it'll be a judgement of God.

How could she accuse that way so sure of herself? Pretend is what they were at, kinder to yard cats nor me, clackin' away to God in their heads like magpies or whisperin' in corners till they're buried separate in God's acre, brides of Christ till they bed down with God Almighty Himself, God help Him. And there goes the Devil makin' me badmind the holy nuns, may God forgive me, but them were happy times forby that one year, happy, happy times till the travellin' tailor called.

—A well-spoken wee fella, Dada said, name of Brady. Thomas Brady. Measured me for a workin' waistcoat. Well fit to read and write, a man with a trade and a share of Latin. He'll be back soon with the waistcoat tailored.

I guessed right off. The match was made and a bad match it was. When Brady come back with the waistcoat it buttoned crooked. Small worry that. But with legs on him like a donkey's foal and no arse worth a mention, that was cause for worry. God help me, I thought, the minute I saw him, do I have to breed with this cratur? Itself is he fit to breed? From the start his trade kept him away, mostly at fairs, or in a tailor's workshop up about Dundalk. Always the smell of whiskey off him when he come back. And the poor mouth. And the excuses. And no money ever.

It was Maggie Scarlett said once,

—Course the like of a travellin' tailor could have weemen here and there.

And, in my own head I thought, Well, if he has, he's left no scatter of childer behind 'cause all he ever planted in me in ten years was one sick caudie, wee Micilín, God help him.

Poor Dada, poor Dada! Them silly girls never quit with their Poor Dada.

Betimes I was near tempted to tell them the way they were planted. A knifegrinder from Kildysart it was. Not a day passes but I think of him. A tall man he was, with good teeth and them heavy-lidded eyes and the soft way they talk down there. Mid-July. Duskus. 1831.

—Have you anythin' needs to be honed, Mam? says he.

—I have, says I. A pair of scissors.

—I can touch them up nicely for you, says he.

—Come in a while, says I. I'm alone in this place.

May God forgive the night I had in the feathers with the knifegrinder. I lost track of who he was and who I was in a fog so blind I didn't give a donkey's howl if they heard me ten townlands away. And when he left at first light and I went down to wash in Callaghan's pool I knew for certain life inside me had begun. Two lives he planted. Never asked him his name. Wild carry on. The Devil was in me that night. He knows his business.

Dada went walkin' to Lough Derg after I married Brady. To shrive his soul and give me a time alone with the bridegroom, God help him.

That first night in the feathers I lay back and laughed at him when he was at his best. Any woman would. The next night, knowin' rightly how the sisters giggled 'bout

The Mother

bein' near split in two by their men, I quit the laughin', opened my legs wide, and said,

—Would you, for God's sake, look at what you're at, man!

You'd swear he was starin' into the mouth of hell with them rabbity eyes.

—What are you afeard of? I asked.

Useless wee shagger, a mickey on him like a thimble and, worse again, a thirst on him for whiskey like an empty still! And the more I'd tongued 'bout how useless he was the more I'd hear them girls whisper,

—Poor Dada. Poor Dada.

And I'd say each time,

—Small loss he's gone, girls, small loss.

Guardian of Virgins. Pray for me.

Pillar of families. Pray for me.

Queen of Confessors. Pray for me.

Never did confess how they were got to a single soul, nor what we were at long ago, half asleep in the straw, tops and tails, boys and girls, and you never knew whose foot was between your legs till the thrill was over and then it was one of the boys with your foot against his thing till it got wet and no one made a sound, may God forgive us, or let on it was goin' on till I asked one day,

—Is it right, this carry on with the feet? What would the clergy make of it? Would the Virgin Mary be at the like?

—Maybe she had no brothers, Cissie said, very shy of herself.

—Clergy have no notion of the like, Sadie said, wicked cross, they're not fit to understand, and you quit this talk, Mary Joe, there's no call for it.

I knew rightly why she wanted the talk to quit. When I was small she'd get me to feel her nipples when her breasts were swellin' pointy. I done this for her and other capers I'd as lief not think or talk about. And why would I? I'm not one for tattle and anyway I'd my own sins to think about, then and now.

Poor Cissie ended up married to the great brute Noel Callaghan. She must be up in heaven now with her three wee girls as sure as Noel's down in hell, and it was our Dada, Holy John, who sent him there, 'cause after a fair at Lisbellaw didn't the same Noel bring home the wida woman from Grencha, Aggie Halpin, a breed of half hoor, the two of them astray in the head from drink. Cissie was too afeard to face them but in dread of what her wee girls might hear or see she got out a windy and come down to our house with her story.

—Go back quick, says Dada, before you're missed, and he carried her story on to Canon McKenna who carried it on to Sergeant Reilly and the two of them lit in on Noel stretched above on the hearth with Halpin astride him wrigglin' hard to plaze him for sixpence.

—Is it your arse in the air now, Jezebel? shouts the Canon givin' her buttocks a woeful lash with his whip.

She screamed and fell off Callaghan and started to crawl for a corner. He follied, whippin' her and shoutin',

—If it's hell you're after, woman, it's hell you'll get from me, bad cess to your filthy trade. I'll name you from the altar, so I will, you blight, you poison, you family polluter, you foul thing in a clean parish! And when she had welts on her as thick as your finger he turned to Callaghan and roared,

—Let that be a lesson to you, Noel Callaghan!

Aye, that's the way of it in this world. It's the men that matter. Two butter balls and a squirty, Father, Son and Holy Ghost. They get off most times with a shout, when the woman gets bate like an ass, 'cause they were hardly out the door when it was Cissie's turn for torture. The brave Noel got her ear till she cringed to her knees.

—Where were you, woman, when I called for me supper? Dancin' over the fields, was it? To whinge off your mouth to the Church and the Law? Was it? And did ya dar' inform on me, ya cunt, ya never give me a man-child yet!

And he took the plough reins from the top of the dresser and every time he lashed Cissie about the kitchen he'd roar time about,

—Where's the Church now? Where's the Law now?

When she come down to our house next day scorched from the plough reins, Mama and we girls cried as she told her story, how Wee Tess was deaf in one ear from a cuff, and how there was always one of her girls bruised or worse, and that was only the half of it 'cause there was other carry on couldn't be spoke of, and the truth is they were all in livin' terror of Noel and most days God sent she said she'd rather be dead and out of it entirely with the angels and saints in heaven. She'd suffered enough. She'd her purgatory done twice over in this world. And who could say other than that?

When Cissie was gone Dada stood listenin' at the half-door as the boys got fierce angry about Callaghan's villainy. We girls joined in and were all noisy at this when he spoke up.

—Quit the talk now, he said. Callaghan's dead.

We all looked at him, his jaw set like a blacksmith's vice. I saw Mama and the girls go white and I'm sure I did too. The three boys were blinkin' hard. No one offered to spake. We all knew he meant what he said.

It was two weeks before Callaghan was fished out of a boghole off our laneway. Dada helped carry his coffin and shovel him under and the Canon preached a sermon 'bout the evils of drink and the mercy of Christ. Poor Noel he said was in trouble with the first and in sore need of the second but most neighbours said,

—It's a wonder to God he lasted so long, the same Noel, but a half miracle for Cissie and her girls now he's gone.

Near the latter end of his life I asked him straight out how Callaghan met his death. He looked at me a brave while before he spoke.

—He was the bad thief, daughter. Christ turned away from the bad thief. So did I.

I knew God told Dada what he must do betimes but to hear it said straight out was a chill to the heart. I accuse he confessed to the clergy, a holy man to be sure, and, true, I'd a great love for him but maybe a greater fear on account of his strictness. A hard judge of men and weemen, but harder again of himself.

—May God forgive me, he said one day, my head's full of nothin' but bad notions.

And the tears come into his eyes, a thing you'd hardly ever see. I asked him how a Christian man as good livin' could be so troubled, and he said,

—The Devil at night, daughter. He poisons the head.

—There's no sin in dreams, I said. Sure the Pope himself has nature like us. He must dream like us, surely to God.

—True enough, he said, only betimes you'd be hard put to know when you're awake and when you're asleep.

That was when I minded a dream wouldn't leave me be, no matter how I prayed or who I prayed to. I tried the Virgin herself, then Brigid, then Monica, and none of them were fit to banish the dream. When I was asleep, down he'd come from the cockloft into the settle bed and I'd take his piesel in my two hands and when I put it inside me it took the breath from me and when we were done he'd crawl out to the street and howl up at the stars like a dog, beggin' God Almighty to forgive him. Then I'd wake in a wet fright to hear him snorin' above and

The Mother

thank God it was a dream only. Even so, I wouldn't be myself all next day.

Maybe it was the like of that had him annoyed. The Devil's a crafty villain and maybe in black dark he planted the same in Dada's head. Who can say? It could never be talked about.

—Bless me, Dada, for I have sinned. My soul's cangled to the Devil on account of —
—What, daughter?
—God knows.
—Tell me.
—Holy God knows all.
—Tell me.
—I can't.
—Then you can't be forgive.
—You're not God, Dada.
—That's where you're wrong.
—You're astray in the head to think you're God.
—The head's more your trouble than mine.

—Got dead, he was, on the road near Pettigo on his way back from that island in Lough Derg where they say it's all circles of Rosaries and rain prayed out over stones in a great red lake, all his sins in the lap of God, and not a one to brag his holiness, or mark his grave, only grass and docks and nettles to redden the arses of angels maybe giggled at the wrong time. Holy John.

No odds much where a body lies in the latter end. Is it? Grave or pit, boneyard or the bottom of the sea. All the one till the trumpet sounds.

May God forgive him just the same for what he done to Noel Callaghan. Bad and all as Noel was he got no chance to make his peace with God, and I've a daughter thinks I done the same to her sister's babby, cold-hearted wee cutty she turned out to be. Did she hear talk maybe 'bout how Dada tipped Callaghan into a boghole? The whole country knew Festus strung up Sammy Agnew like a fox, and if that was father and son then, maybe, she'd think me well fit to block out the life of a wee innocent. And maybe the same badness is in her too. Said she'd kill me and meant it, so she did, and when I shaped to tell her different times she screamed back at me, her two fingers in her two ears. I quit tryin'. I wasn't goin' to beg a hearin' from my own blood. I'm proud too. And that one time she come here and kissed my hands I thought, I'll tell her now. I couldn't. Not with that look in her face and now she'll never hear what was in my head to say.

I was half cracked with grief that time, daughter, but no murderer. I chained up your sister's shame to hide it 'cause I'm cangled to shame myself, chained her in fright and sorrow with mad-eyed hunger and death starin' into every other cabin. I'll not deny what I done but give me a second chance I'd have marched her round the neighbours all and bared her belly to the sun and shouted out,

—Look, my daughter Grace is full of life. God's work, and God is good, is He not? God'll mind us. God'll send down food from heaven. God is kinder surely than Murphy, the Master of this poorhouse, is He not? Is He?

Sadie it was first brought news of that Murphy fella to Drumlanna, that time she was bonded out to Fergusons. Full of him she was, the workin' boy steward, a skelp of Lord Skinner's, some said, but whatever he was she'd fair sicken you talkin' 'bout the lovely voice of him, and oh the laugh of him, and oh the jokes of him, and oh the way he could sit a horse, and oh the way he could talk aisy with gentry or country folk and how all the byre girls were wet for him. She was that much of a dose I asked her once,

—Were you wet for him, Sadie, did he sit on you?

—Ya jealous lump, she said. Whatever he done with me

The Mother

he wouldn'a done with you. No man with an eye in his head'd bother with a hallion like you.

And straight back to her face I said,

—One cunt's as good as another in the dark.

Oh she fair screamed out her temper and scrabbed my face with her nails and we never spoke aisy from that day till she married nor for long after, nor her childer to mine, and me closer to her growin' up than any of the others. Not a secret between us. And now she's buried in the ocean deep, the half of her childer down there with her. God, how I loved her long ago! May Christ have mercy on her soul at the bottom of the sea. It's far she is now from byre kisses and the larks of Bragan. Oh Jesus, why do we human families torture other the way we do? A silly grig from me, a bad tempered scrab from her, and then the long bitterness. Oh Sadie, if you came to me now smilin' from the bottom of the sea I'd throw my two arms round you and cry hot tears for all them years we lost hatin' other over the head of nothin'. Better again, if my Roisin come back for five minutes and listened to my story and believed it I'd die happy. Stood across from me at Grace's grave, so she did, and when the first shovel dundered on the boards that near stopped my heart with grief I looked up and saw her face all glares and stares forninst me. Hatred, or near enough, writ all over it. My own daughter. Neighbours I half knew gave me more comfort.

Oh my love, my love, my Roisin Dubh, wherever you're gone remember me kindly,

I'd walk the dew beside you, or the bitter desert

In hopes I might merit a smile of your love.

Fragrant branch of mine, give me word, let me hope,

O choicest flower of Ireland, my Roisin Dubh.

Have pity on your poor mother and may the Mother of God have pity on the fruit of my womb, my dead daughter Grace, and the dead-born fruit of her womb. Ask your Son to forgive her, and me, your disgraced servant, Mary Josephine, all our sins.

God help me, God help me, God help me.

Out of the depths I have cried unto thee, O Lord.

Lord, hear my voice, because with Thee, Lord, there is mercy, with Thee there is plentiful redemption. With Thee there is forgiveness. Aye, but hunger too!

The pity was I didn't die in the briars of Scart that time I was crazed. Die and be done with it. What had we to live for, the most of us? Not a bite in the house bar England's charity, the stirabout of India meal. A dose of the skitters, they sent us, gravel and shite, and their great ships sailin' from our ports half foundered with food from every townland of Ireland to feed their murderin' armies at the four ends of the earth. May they suffer some day for what they done to us. And where was Tom Brady, the bespoke tailor, left us in our time of need? Piss blind in Dundalk.

—Small loss he's gone, girls, I said every time. Small loss. I'd as lief we'd all starve and be ghosts ourselves as see aither of you plump at Drumbofin! Scullions to Bob Skinner, Lord Clonroy, is it? Ride whatever's handy, them gentry, high or low, man or woman, boy or girl, calf or nanny goat, up and in and jiggle away till their wee fit's over. May the Devil fuck them! Oh God, forgive my tongue but may He double fuck them down to hell, and his hired brutes skewered us for rent of land was ours, that tumbled us into the jaws of winter when the praties failed, that left us without sow or cow, calf or clucking hen, that tipped my flax-wheel and my stool, my poor pillows of meadowsweet, like dead things into a sheugh, whose flunkeys cut my nightlines set for jack pikes in the lough at Tirnahinch, that took the sleep from me, and the hope from me, and my house from me, and my family

The Mother

from me, and my wits from me, that robbed me of the sweet mint from the hill of Corduff, that left me naked in the bog of Scart astray in the head and chewin' on bitter sorrel. Oh Christ the Judge, there's no forgivin' the like, none now, or ever more, Amen.

Ah my love, my love, my Roisin Dubh, if you'd come to me you'd have heard the way it was that night and no one in it only myself in a blind of terror, that night you ran away when the babby was caught at the shoulders for hours and dead for hours, and I callin' every minute on God above to help me before I dragged it from her body by its neck and then the great bloodfall and me on my knees watchin' the life go out of my own poor cratur, dyin', dyin' like a candle, before my eyes.

And after that in deep sleep I seen her free herself from the chain and run down through the night with her babby to Callaghan's pool and heerd her voice and her wee thing cryin' out in the black dark. Near broke my heart 'cause she'd nothin' in her belly, and how could she have milk in her breasts to feed the babby, and I was runnin' and runnin' and shoutin',

—They'll die, they'll die, they'll drown theirselves, my daughter, oh my daughter, my poor, poor daughter, don't do it, Grace, for the love of God, and the Blessèd Virgin, don't do it. And another voice in my head was sayin',

—They'll come to no harm, no harm at all, God'll mind them.

Aye, surely, but the Devil's know'd my story and where do you look for two lost angels in the dark when that's what you're up agin'? And I was sarchin' and sarchin' in sheughs and vennels all thorn scrabbed, tore and bloody, with no notion in the world they were dead. Gone now, Grace and her wee blue-faced bundle, dead, gone, buried and forgot! Forgot? No mercy then or now. I was in hell that night that last time you come here and

I sarchin' for words to begin my story when you said of a sudden,

—May God forgive you, Mama, I never will.

And walked away from here with your bag and your boat ticket, and that Murphy man locked the door and me screamin' and screamin' out through the windy,

—Don't lave me here to die, daughter, for the love of Jesus Christ, have pity on your poor mother. Don't lave me.

And you walked on across that big yard through ghosty paupers, out and away through them big gates, forever and ever. And never once looked back.

Virgin most merciful, I'll die alone in this place now and, if that's how my story ends, be with me at the end. And be with me now through this day. Help sweeten my thoughts and soften my tongue. Give me back the old, rounded days of nature long ago when we had the black cow with the white nose and the garden of lumpers every year on the south hill under Carn, and I watchin' Dada dig them in or shovel them out and bag more than enough to feed us all, and the odd beggar too, and the scatter of hens, and a pig betimes, and oaten bread from the cut of oats, and every year come early May, bright or hasky, we'd be off to the red bog of Bragan to save turf and Dada was God and Mama was love with buttermilk and cold pandy and she made tay from a heather bruss in a can and I was a wee thing in a bag skirt playin' happy and laughin' with the others, and that bog bank was heaven, so it was, heaven, with the shower of larks high over our heads that never quit singin' and singin' and singin'.

Acknowledgements

Tales from the Poorhouse (and its translation into Irish by John McArdle, *Scéalta Ó Theach na mBocht*) was commissioned by Teilifís na Gaeilge and RTE, with assistance from Bord Scannán na hÉireann. A Crescendo Concept, produced and directed by Louis Lentin. The television versions, in Irish and English, feature the following cast:

THE ORPHAN	Sheenagh Walsh
THE MASTER	Brendan Gleeson
THE LANDLORD	Mick Lally
THE MOTHER	Ruth McCabe

Sources

Unpublished
   Minutes from Armagh and Lurgan poorhouses 1848

Published
   Thomas Gallagher, *Paddy's Lament: Ireland 1846-47. Prelude to Hatred*
   John Killen, *The Famine Decade, Contemporary Accounts, 1841-51*
   George Moore, *The Untilled Field*
   Frank O'Connor, *A Book of Ireland*
   John O'Connor, *The Workhouses of Ireland*
   Seán Ó Tuama and Thomas Kinsella, *An Duanaire: Poems of the Dispossessed 1600-1900*
   Cathal Portéir, *Famine Echoes*
   David Thompson, *Woodbrook*